学术顾问
（以姓氏笔画为序）

王　宏　　冯智文　　李正栓　　李丽生　　原一川

Academic Advisors
Wang Hong　　Feng Zhiwen　　Li Zhengshuan
Li Lisheng　　Yuan Yichuan

主　编
李昌银

副主编
黄　瑛　　彭庆华

General Editor
Li Changyin

Professor of English　　Yunnan Normal University

Associate General Editors
Huang Ying

Professor of English　　Yunnan Normal University

Peng Qinghua

Professor of English　　Yunnan Normal University

云南少数民族经典作品英译文库
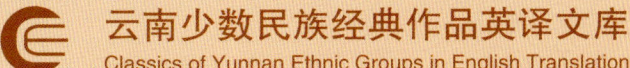
Classics of Yunnan Ethnic Groups in English Translation

主编　李昌银　General Editor　Li Changyin
副主编　黄瑛　彭庆华　Associate General Editors　Huang Ying & Peng Qinghua

The War Between the Black and the White Tribes
黑白之战

整理◎杨世光
英译◎孙兴文　贾丽丽　罗慧凡
译校◎[美]包琼

Edited by Yang Shiguang
Translated by Sun Xingwen,
Jia Lili & Luo Huifan
Revised by Joan Cecile Boulerice

云南出版集团
云南人民出版社

图书在版编目（CIP）数据

黑白之战：汉、英 / 杨世光整理；孙兴文，贾丽丽，罗慧凡英译. -- 昆明：云南人民出版社，2020.2
（云南少数民族经典作品英译文库 / 李昌银主编）
ISBN 978-7-222-19073-3

Ⅰ.①黑… Ⅱ.①杨… ②孙… ③贾… ④罗… Ⅲ.①纳西族—民间故事—中国—汉、英 Ⅳ.①I277.3

中国版本图书馆CIP数据核字(2020)第028253号

出 品 人	李　维　　赵石定
项目统筹	周　祥　　殷筱钊
项目组稿	郭木玉
责任编辑	郭木玉　　费　珺
装帧设计	马　滨　　石　斌
责任校对	明　珍　　王琳淇　　溥　思
责任印制	陆卫华　　代隆参

云南少数民族经典作品英译文库
Classics of Yunnan Ethnic Groups in English Translation

黑白之战
The War Between the Black and the White Tribes

整理◎杨世光
英译◎孙兴文　贾丽丽　罗慧凡
译校◎[美]包琼

Edited by Yang Shiguang
Translated by Sun Xingwen, Jia Lili & Luo Huifan
Revised by Joan Cecile Boulerice

出　　版	云南出版集团　云南人民出版社
发　　行	云南人民出版社
社　　址	昆明市环城西路609号
邮　　编	650034
网　　址	www.ynpph.com.cn
E-mail	ynrms@sina.com
开　　本	787mm×1092mm　1/16
印　　张	20
字　　数	272千
版　　次	2020年2月第1版第1次印刷
印　　刷	云南出版印刷集团有限责任公司　云南新华印刷一厂
书　　号	978-7-222-19073-3
定　　价	110.00元

云南人民出版社
微信公众号

序 一

◎李正栓

民族典籍英译是传播中国文化、文学和文明的重要途径，是中华文化走出去的重要组成部分。文化与文学的传播，是一个国家提高文化软实力的重要方式，在文化交流和文明建设中起着不可或缺的作用，对提高国家对外话语权、构建国家对外话语体系以及对建设世界文学都有积极意义。

中国各少数民族拥有许多优秀的典籍，具有很高的文物价值、文学价值和文化价值。各民族的先人们通过口头流传或用文字记述了他们各具特色的文化。各少数民族几乎都有自己民族的创世史、史诗和神话传说。

中国民族典籍独具特色，不可替代。重视民族典籍的翻译和研究工作，对于挖掘各民族优秀文化，保护各民族文明，增强各民族之间的沟通和了解，进一步向世界其他地区传播各少数民族优秀文化，乃至提高我国文化软实力都有着重要意义。不少少数民族聚居地处于祖国边疆，有的处在"一带一路"建设关键部位，有的处在与周边国家进行各种交流的重要位置。

中国民族典籍是世界多元文化的有机组成部分，与其他文化共同造就了世界文化的绚丽多姿。世界正因为其文化多样性才变得缤纷多彩。我国各民族典籍中包含的文化多样性极大地丰富了世界多元、特色鲜明的文化。人们对多样性形成全新的认识角度和思维方式。多样性开阔了人们的视野，丰富了人们思考问题的角度。挖掘这些典籍中所蕴含的教育价值和文化价值，对世界其他民族都有指导和借鉴意义，并且有助于建设我国的文化自信。

民族典籍本身蕴含的特殊价值对加强民族文化了解、促进中外文化交流具有重大意义。民族典籍英译具有文学翻译和文化传递之功能，有对外宣传作用，还是一种文学外交。因此，民族典籍翻译和研究对于维护祖国统一、促进民族团结、稳定边疆以及增强国内各民族和中外文化之间的交流都起着极为重要的作用。

中华人民共和国成立以后，中央政府一直十分重视民族典籍翻译和研究工作，提供了强有力的政策支持，并采取了一系列有效措施，加快了各少数民族典籍的抢救、整理、翻译和研究的进程。中央政府多次召开西藏工作会议和新疆工作会议。近年来，国际和国内对于多元文化高度关注，少数民族文学典籍的翻译已然成为业内研究的热点。

近年来，民族典籍翻译和研究迅猛发展，势头良好。国家大力支持，发放国家社科基金课题，教育部和国家民委也发放课题，扶持了一大批研究者。很多民族典籍翻译课题得以立项并顺利开展；为数不少的民族典籍被翻译成汉语、英语和其他语言并出版发行；越来越多的业界人士致力于这个满富生机的学术领域。

在中国文化走出去的国家战略下，全国少数民族典籍英译学术研讨会陆续召开，已经召开三次。

云南是中国民族最多的省份。人口在 5000 人以上的少数民族有 25 个，其中有 15 个民族为云南所特有，分别是：白族、哈尼族、傣族、傈僳族、佤族、拉祜族、纳西族、景颇族、布朗族、普米族、阿昌族、基诺族、怒族、德昂族、独龙族。其中除白族人口占全国白族人口总数的 84% 以上外，其他 14 个民族 95% 居住在云南。

云南还是我国跨境民族最多的省份。在云南的 25 个少数民族中，有 16 个民族跨境而居，分别是：傣族、壮族、苗族、景颇族、瑶族、哈尼族、德昂族、佤族、拉祜族、彝族、阿昌族、傈僳族、布依族、怒族、布朗族、独龙族。

云南少数民族创造了辉煌的文化。据不完全统计，云南少数民族文字文献古籍蕴藏量达 10 万余册（卷），口传古籍 4 万余种。云南省民委少数民族古籍整理出版规划办公室为了挽救和保护这些古籍，计划在 5 年内编纂出版 100 卷《云南少数民族古籍珍本集成》。这是一个令人瞩目的庞大计划。将这些古籍中的珍品翻译介绍给世界，不仅能够弘扬云南省丰富多彩的民族文化，而且有助于增进与南亚东南亚国家的理解与交流，为"一带一路"倡议的实施做出贡献。

云南师范大学外国语学院很重视这一领域的工作。在外国语学院领导支持下，李昌银教授带领一个由教授和中青年学者组成的团队对精选出来的 17 部云南少数民族经典作品进行英译，计划在 5 年内（"十三五"期间）翻译出版。这是一项十分有意义的宏大工程。

这 17 部民族典籍，内容全部为各民族的英雄史诗或神话传说，具有很高的历史意义和文学价值。这些作品涉及阿昌族、白族、傣族、德昂族、哈尼族、景颇族、拉祜族、苗族、纳西族、普米族、彝族等11个少数民族。

云南师范大学这支翻译队伍实力强大，主要由一些多年从事翻译教学、研究和实践的教授和副教授组成，他们是李昌银、黄瑛、彭庆华、孙兴文、吴相如、刘德周、杨慧芳、郜菊、陈萍、包琼（Joan Cecile Boulerice）等国内外专家学者。他们在云南翻译界都是风云人物。

在民族典籍英译中，这支队伍异军突起，为我国民族典籍英译壮大了声势，必将为中国民族典籍走向世界而成为世界文学的一部分做出新贡献。

民族典籍翻译与研究事业关乎国家的稳定统一，关乎民族关系的和谐发展，关乎世界多元文化的实现。在中国，民族典籍资源极为丰富，有待进一步挖掘、翻译。因此，民族典籍英译前景光明。同时，我们也应意识到，仍有许多濒临消失的少数民族典籍亟待拯救，民族典籍翻译与研究工作任重而道远。

（李正栓，中国英汉语比较研究会典籍英译专业委员会常务副会长兼秘书长、河北师范大学博士生导师）

Foreword by Li Zhengshuan

The translation of Chinese ethnic classics is an important approach in spreading Chinese culture, literature and civilization. It is a crucial component of Chinese culture going global. The spreading of Chinese culture and literature is a national policy and an important way to improve the cultural soft power of China. It plays an indispensable role in the cultural exchange between China and other countries and the development of world literature.

The ethnic groups in China have countless excellent classics with high anthropological, literary and cultural value. The ancestors of each ethnic group have passed down their distinctive culture orally or in writing. Almost all the ethnic groups have their own story of creation, epics, myths and legends.

Chinese ethnic classics are unique and irreplaceable. It is imperative to attach importance to the translation and research of ethnic classics; to explore the excellent ethnic cultures; to protect the civilization of ethnic groups; to enhance the communication and understanding among ethnic groups; to further spread the outstanding culture of ethnic groups to other parts of the world; and to build the cultural strength of China. Many ethnic groups live in the border areas and thus play an important role in the cultural and economic cooperation between China and its neighbors in the context of the Belt and Road Initiative.

Chinese ethnic classics are an important component of the magnificence and diversity of world culture. It is diversity that makes the world so colorful. The cultural diversity of Chinese ethnic classics has greatly enriched the world's pluralism and its distinctive features. People around the world have formed a new understanding of diversity. This diversity has expanded people's horizon and enriched their way of thinking. Digging out the educational and cultural value in these classics can contribute to the construction of China's self-confidence in culture.

The special value of the ethnic classics itself is of great significance to the strengthening of national culture and intercultural communication between China and foreign countries. The translation of ethnic classics is not just a literary exchange, but also a form of cultural communication. It is diplomacy through literature in that it consolidates the cultural ties between China and other countries.

After the founding of the People's Republic of China, the central government attached great importance to the translation and research of ethnic classics, provided a great deal of policy support, and adopted a series of effective measures to speed up the process of rescuing, collating, translating and studying ethnic classics. The central government has convened several working conferences on Tibet and Xinjiang. In recent years, both China and other countries have paid close attention to multiculture. The translation of ethnic classics has become a hot topic.

In recent years, the translation and research of ethnic classics have progressed rapidly and have shown good prospects. The government strongly supports and grants the research projects of the national social science fund. The Ministry of Education and the State Ethnic Affairs Commission are also issuing research projects and giving funding to a large number of researchers. Many research projects on ethnic classics have been approved and carried out. Many ethnic classics have been translated into Chinese, English and other languages and published. More and more professionals have dedicated themselves to this new sphere of learning.

In this context, the academic conferences on translation of ethnic classics are held one after another all around the country. And up to now three have been held.

Yunnan is the province which has the most ethnic groups in China. Besides the Han people, there are 25 ethnic groups, each with a population of more than 5,000. Among them, 15 ethnic groups are unique to Yunnan, which are the Bai, the Hani, the Dai, the Lisu, the Wa, the Lahu, the Naxi, the Jingpo, the Bulang, the Pumi, the Achang, the Jinuo, the Nu, the De'ang and the Dulong. Among these, 84% of the total number of the Bai people in China and 95% of the other 14 ethnic groups are living in Yunnan.

Yunnan is also the province which has the most cross-border ethnic groups. Of the 25 ethnic groups, 16 live across the border, namely: the Dai, the Zhuang, the Miao, the Jingpo, the Yao, the Hani, the De'ang, the Wa, the Lahu, the Yi, the Achang, the Lisu, the Buyi, the Nu, the Bulang and the Dulong.

The ethnic groups in Yunnan have created splendid cultures. According to statistics, the number of classics of Yunnan ethnic groups is more than 100 thousand volumes and classics in oral tradition are more than 40 thousand. In order to save and protect these ancient books, the Office of Classics Collation and Publishing of Yunnan Ethnic Groups Affairs Commission planned to compile and publish 100 volumes of *A Collection of Yunnan Ethnic Group Rare Books* in five years, which is an ambitious plan. The introduction of the ancient classics via translation can not only promote and develop the colorful ethnic cultures of Yunnan, but also contribute to the understanding and exchange between China and countries in South Asia and Southeast Asia and to the implementation of the Belt and Road Initiative as well.

The School of Foreign Languages and Literature of Yunnan Normal University is paying close attention to this field. With the support of the School and the University,

Professor Li Changyin is leading a group of professors and young scholars to do the project of *Classics of Yunnan Ethnic Groups in English Translation*, which includes 17 ethnic classics selected carefully from Yunnan's bountiful ethnic classics. These books are the heroic epics or myths and legends of each ethnic groups with great historical significance and literary value. They will finish the translation in five years (during the Thirteenth Five-Year Plan). After that, all the works will be published by Yunnan People's Publishing House.

The 17 works cover 11 ethnic groups: the Achang, the Bai, the Dai, the De'ang, the Hani, the Jingpo, the Lahu, the Miao, the Naxi, the Pumi and the Yi. All of these groups except the Miao and the Yi are unique to Yunnan.

The translation team of Yunnan Normal University is full of strength and vitality, composed of professors and associate professors who have been occupied in translation teaching, research, and practice for a long time. They are Li Changyin, Huang Ying, Peng Qinghua, Sun Xingwen, Wu Xiangru, Liu Dezhou, Yang Huifang, Gao Ju, Chen Ping, Joan Boulerice and other experts and scholars who are representative figures in the translation field in Yunnan province.

This team is a new force that has suddenly arisen in terms of translating ethnic classics. It is expanding the momentum of ethnic classics translation in China and has made a new contribution for China's ethnic classics to go global and become a part of world literature.

The translation and research of ethnic classics are related to the development of Chinese culture and the realization of multiculturalism in the world. In China, ethnic classics are extremely rich in resources, which require us to make further exploration and research and translate them into other languages. Therefore, the future of translating ethnic classics is bright. At the same time, we should also realize that there are still many ethnic works which are close to extinction and urgently need to be rescued. We still have a long way to go in the fields of translation and research in ethnic classics.

(Li Zhengshuan, Standing Vice Chairman and Secretary General, Classics Translation Committee of CACSEC, PhD supervisor at Hebei Normal University)

序 二

◎王 宏

好友云南师范大学外国语学院李昌银教授来电嘱托我为"云南少数民族经典作品英译文库"的出版写一序言,并随即发来该文库的背景资料,让我"不着急,慢慢写"。我本人从事中国典籍英译及研究,深知少数民族典籍对外传译的重要性,但又是少数民族典籍翻译的门外汉。因此,我是怀着虚心学习的态度来写此序言的。近年来,在中国文化"走出去"战略工程大背景下,在中央和地方各级政府的大力支持下,我国少数民族典籍的对外传译及研究工作顺利开展,取得了很大的进步。请看以下数据:

2008年,广西百色学院韩家权教授获批国家社科基金项目《布洛陀史诗》(壮汉英对照)。该项目已顺利结项,并于2013年12月获得中国民间文艺最高奖"山花奖"。

2012年,广西百色学院外语系翻译团队翻译的国家级非物质文化遗产《壮族嘹歌》(英文版)由广西师范大学出版社正式出版。

2012年,东北大学秦皇岛分校吴松林教授主编的《蒙古族系列:江格尔(汉英对照)》(上下册)由吉林大学出版社出版。

2013年,河北师范大学李正栓教授英译《藏族格言诗》

由长春出版社出版发行。

2013年，云南财经大学崔晓霞教授撰写的《〈阿诗玛〉英译研究》收入由王宏印教授主编、民族出版社出版的"民族典籍翻译研究丛书"。

2014年，东北大学秦皇岛分校吴松林教授撰写的《满族档案文献研究》申请到国家社科后期资助，他英译的《英雄格斯尔可汗》由吉林大学出版社出版。

2014年，中南民族大学张立玉教授主持的"土家族主要典籍英译及研究"获批国家社科基金项目。

2015年，西安外国语大学梁真惠副教授撰写的《〈玛纳斯〉翻译传播研究》收入由王宏印教授主编、民族出版社出版的"民族典籍翻译研究丛书"。

与此同时，第一届和第二届全国少数民族典籍英译学术研讨会分别于2012年和2014年在广西民族大学和大连民族学院举行，参加会议的院校分布之广、与会代表数量之众、提交论文数量之多和涉及研究话题之细，十分可喜。2016年还将在中南民族大学举行第三届全国少数民族典籍英译学术研讨会。

为什么少数民族典籍的对外传译及研究工作在短短几年就受到译界的青睐，取得众多成果？我认为，这在很大程度上归于典籍翻译界乃至翻译界同仁对"中国典籍"的重新思考和认识。中国典籍浩如烟海，卷帙浩繁，举世瞩目，是全人类共同的精神财富。但对于中国典籍的理解，我们以前较多限于汉民族的重要文献和书籍，而对少数民族多有忽略。在讨论中国典籍时，也较多关注古代文学作品。其实，中国典籍指"中国清代末年1911年以前的重要文献和书籍",这就要求我们从事典籍翻译时,不但要翻译古代文学典籍作品,还要翻译古代哲学、科技、法律、医学、经济、军事、天文、地理等诸多方面的典籍作品,不但要翻译汉民族的典籍作品,也要翻译各少数民族的典籍作品。

民族典籍具有该民族的原型符号的特质,蕴藏着能够"遗传"并不断"再生"的文化基因。民族典籍是中华传统文化的内核,同时还是中华传统文化的符号构成规则。中国是具有56个民族的多民族国家,少数民族典籍是我国少数民族勤劳与智慧的结晶,是中华文明、也是世界文明不可或缺的一部分。少数民族典籍对外传译具有跨文化交流的作用,它不但有助于更多的人了解少数民族的独特文化,而且还有助于保护少数民族文化的独特性、维持少数民族文化多样性、促进各民族团结、提升中华文化软实力等。

中国少数民族典籍涉及宗教、文学、历史、语言、医学、天文历算等领域,内容丰富,版本多样,载体特殊,传承奇特。仅以《中国少数民族古籍总目提要》为例,该书于1997年正式立项,全书总体设计约60卷、110册,目前已出版23个民族卷共20册:纳西族卷、白族卷、东乡族卷·裕固族卷·保安族卷、土族卷·撒拉族卷、锡伯族卷、哈尼族卷、回族卷·铭刻、柯尔克孜族卷、羌族卷、毛南族卷·京族卷、仫佬族卷、达斡尔族卷、土家族卷、鄂温克族卷、鄂伦春族卷、赫哲族卷、苗族卷、侗族卷、黎族卷、朝鲜族卷。该书真实地反映了我国各少数民族古籍赋存的全面情况,充实了中国的历史和文化内容,为后人探索各种文化形式的源流、揭示中国社会文化发展的轨迹提供了极为珍贵的资料，为我国乃至世界各国人文科学研究提供了一套新颖而全面的资料，对于弘扬中华民族传统文化具有深远的历史意义和现实意义。

少数民族典籍的对外传译是一项艰巨的工作，涉及将少数民族语言译成汉语、少数民族语言之间的互译和少数民族语言译成外语（主要是英语）。前两类翻译历史源远流长，最早可追溯到春秋战国时代《越人歌》的翻译，即汉、壮语之间的翻译。少数民族典籍译成外语的时间则要晚一些。据考证，维吾尔族古典长诗《福乐智慧》成书于1069年或1070年，目前尚未发现完整的原稿，只存留下来三个抄本，分别为赫拉特抄本、费尔干纳抄本与埃及抄本，其中费尔干纳抄本于12~13世纪用阿拉伯文纳斯赫体抄写，1914年发现于今中亚乌孜别克斯坦纳曼干城，现存于该共和国科学院东方研究所。这是少数民族典籍译介到国外的最早纪录。少数民族典籍外译在现代有了较快发展。一些少数民族典籍，如藏族的《格萨尔王传》、蒙古族的《江格尔》和柯尔克孜族的《玛纳斯》等英雄史诗，云南彝族的《阿诗玛》、维吾尔族的《艾里甫和赛乃姆》等民间叙事长诗已先后被翻译成英语及其他外国文字，为世人所知。这对传承少数民族经典，推动中外文化交流起到了不可替代的作用。然而，还有大量的中国少数民族典籍等待我们去翻译和研究。

云南省少数民族典籍资源十分丰富。据不完全统计，云南少数民族文字文献古籍蕴藏量达10万余册（卷），口传古籍4万余种。"云南少数民族经典作品英译文库"正是依托云南省丰富的少数民族典籍资源，借助云南师范大学外国语学院强大的翻译师资队伍，在云南人民出版社的有力支持下，首次将云南少数民族经典作品成系列对外译介的大力举措。云南师范大学外国语学院对"云南少数民族经典作品英译文库"十分重视，他们首先邀请省内外少数民族语言文化研究专家对云南民族典籍和民族文化经典作品进行筛选，做到"好中选好，优中选优"，同时调配最强的翻译力量承担文库的翻译任务。我粗略看了该文库的选题，发现选题面广，覆盖范围宽，收入了云南省阿昌族、白族、傣族、纳西族、德昂族、哈尼族、景颇族、拉祜族、苗族、普米族和彝族等民族的典籍作品。云南共有25个少数民族，其中11个少数民族的典籍作品都覆盖到了，不少作品还是首次译成英文。这将彻底改变云南少数民族典籍由于对外译介数量较少，不为世界了解的尴尬局面。

对于云南师范大学外国语学院而言，把少数民族典籍英译作为翻译专业的优势特色进行建设，这将对该院的学科建设起到助推作用。"云南少数民族经典作品英译文库"所产生的翻译成果和研究成果将培养出一批优秀的典籍翻译和研究团队，凸显该院在全国的学术特色和学术影响，同时还能将翻译能力和研究能力转化为教学能力，提高云南师范大学外国语学院翻译专业研究生的培养质量，为社会输送高水平的翻译人才，有力地支撑学院翻译专业学科的建设和发展。我对云南师范大学外国语学院的翻译师资队伍较为熟悉。作为云南省唯一获得省级高校优势特色学科建设项目的外国语学院，该院具有雄厚的翻译师资力量，在云南省各高校中当属第一。多年来，该院翻译与跨文化研究团队一直承担着对外交流与合作的各种口笔译项目及任务。由外国语学院精心挑选和确定的"云南少数民族经典作品英译文库"翻译人员绝大多数都是云南省翻译领域里的知名教授或专家，有国外留学经历，且具有扎实的英汉双语语言功底，曾翻译出版多部译著和翻译作品，并且主持和参与过多项翻译项目的研究。我阅读李昌银教授发来的文库翻译人员名单，发现多名我所熟悉的知名教授、博士也在其中，感到格外放心。

"云南少数民族经典作品英译文库"的出版发行是云南省翻译界的一件大事，也是我国少数民族典籍翻译传来的又一佳音。想当年，我和"大中华文库"总协调人李林老师曾在参加全国典籍英译学术研讨会之余一起找到李昌银教授，敦促李教授向学校和同事呼吁，少数民族典籍翻译及研究是富矿，值得快挖、深挖，能早出成果，出大成果。今天，我们当年的心愿变成了美好的现实，心里感到特别高兴。再次热烈祝贺"云南少数民族经典作品英译文库"的顺利出版！

（王宏，中国典籍翻译研究会副会长、苏州大学博士生导师）

Foreword by Wang Hong

My friend Professor Li Changyin of Yunnan Normal University asked me to write a few words for the publication of *Classics of Yunnan Ethnic Groups in English Translation*. I am more than delighted to do it. As I have been doing research in English translation of Chinese classics, I know how important this work is. In recent years, substantial progress has been made in translating Chinese ethnic classics into English and introducing them to the world. Let's look at the following accomplishments.

First of all, several projects in the English translation of ethnic classics have received funding from the National Planning Office of Philosophy and Social Science. The first of these projects is *The Epic of Baeuqloxgdoh* (Zhuang-Chinese-English trilingual version), given funding in 2008 and headed by Professor Han Jiaquan of Baise University in Guangxi Zhuang Autonomous Region. In December 2013, this translation won the Shanhua Award, the most prestigious prize for folk literature and art in China. The second project is *A Study of the Manchu Archives*, written by Professor Wu Songlin of Northeastern University at Qinhuangdao and which was given funding in 2014. The third is *English*

Translation and Study of the Major Classics of the Tujia Ethnic Group, headed by Professor Zhang Liyu of the South-Central University for Nationalities, also granted in 2014.

Secondly, several English translations have been published. In 2012, *Liao Songs of Pingguo Zhuang*, has been listed as one of China's national intangible cultural heritages. It was translated by the School of Foreign Languages, Baise University, and published by Guangxi Normal University Press. Also in 2012, *Jangar* (a Chinese-English bilingual edition), edited by Professor Wu Songlin of Northeastern University at Qinhuangdao, was published by Jilin University Press. In 2013, *Tibetan Gnomic Verses Translated into English*, translated by Professor Li Zhengshuan of Hebei Normal University, was published by Changchun Press. And in 2014, *Heroic Geser Khan*, translated by Professor Wu Songlin of Northeastern University at Qinhuangdao, was published by Jilin University Press.

And thirdly, two important monographs have been published by The Ethnic Publishing House in the *Ethnic Classics Translation Research Series* edited by Professor Wang Hongyin of Nankai University. One is *A Study on the English Translation of* Ashima *by Gladys Taylor* (2013), which was the PhD dissertation of Professor Cui Xiaoxia of Yunnan University of Finance and Economics. The other is *Translation and Dissemination of the Oral Epic Manas* (2015) written by Associate Professor Liang Zhenhui of Xi'an International

Studies University.

Meanwhile, it is encouraging to see that the first conferences on English translation of ethnic classics in China have been held in Guangxi Nationalities University and Dalian Nationalities Institute respectively. Participants were both many and enthusiastic. Many papers were presented and a lot of topics discussed. The third conference will be hosted by South Central Nationalities University in 2016.

Why, then, has this field attracted so much attention from translators and scholars alike and accomplished so much in just a few years? The answer, I believe, lies in a rethinking of what constitutes Chinese classics as an indispensable part of human heritage. We used to see Chinese classics as more or less equal to the classics of the Han people, excluding works by other ethnic groups. Moreover, when we talk about Chinese classics, we focus too much on the literary works of ancient times. Yet Chinese classics actually refer to "important works and books before 1911, the year when the Qing dynasty fell, bringing an end to imperial rule". This definition requires us to pay attention not just to literary works, but also writings in other subjects, such as philosophy, science, law, medicine, economics, military affairs, astronomy, and geography, not only Han works, but writings by other ethnic groups as well.

The classical works of a nation are its archetypal symbols, the major carriers of its cultural genes. Chinese classics make up the core of Chinese tradition. The Chinese nation consists of 56 ethnic groups. Ethnic classics are an important part of not only Chinese traditional culture, but also world civilization. The translation of these works into other languages is important in that it helps to promote cross-cultural communications between China and other countries and to protect and preserve the uniqueness and diversity of ethnic cultures by making them accessible to foreign readers.

Chinese ethnic classics cover a variety of areas, such as religion, literature, history, language, medicine, astrology, and calendar, with numerous editions, special media and unique ways of transmission from generation to generation. Take, for example, *An Anthology of Chinese Ethnic Classics*, a colossal project that includes 110 volumes, 20 of which, from 23 ethnic groups, have been published. The anthology reflects the variety and quantity of China's ethnic classics and provides valuable material and resources for studying, understanding and developing Chinese culture and history in a more comprehensive and sustainable way.

The translation of Chinese ethnic classics into foreign languages is a very demanding job, involving rendering from ethnic languages to Chinese, between ethnic languages, and from ethnic languages (often via Chinese) to foreign languages. The first two types of translation can be traced back to the Spring and Autumn Period, when *The Song of the Yue People* was translated from their mother tongue into Chinese. The earliest translation of ethnic classics into a foreign language is *Wisdom of Royal Glory*, a long poem of the Uygurs, which was rendered from the source language into Arabic and is now in the Oriental Institute of Uzbekistan at Namangan. But it was not until modern times that the translation of ethnic classics into foreign languages accelerated. Noticeably, ethnic epics, such as *The Story of Prince Geser* of the Tibetans, *The Story of Jianggeer* of the Mongolians, *Manas* of the Kyrgyz, and narrative poems such as *Ashima* of the Yi people, *Alip and Salam* of the Uygurs, etc., have been published. These translations have contributed to acquainting the world with Chinese ethnic classics, but many remain to be translated.

Yunnan is rich in ethnic classics, boasting more than 100,000 volumes of written classics and over 40,000 pieces of oral literature. Relying on such bountiful resources, as a collective endeavor of the translation team of the School of Foreign Languages and Literature, Yunnan Normal University and with the help of Yunnan People's Publishing House, *Classics of Yunnan Ethnic Groups in English Translation* is the first project to translate Yunnan ethnic classics into English on a large scale. The School adheres to a professional spirit and academic standard in carrying out the project by selecting the most authoritative texts in the source language (Chinese) and recruiting the best translators from its huge faculty. The selection of the works, covering eleven of the twenty-five ethnic groups of the province, indicates expertise and insight. The implementation of the project will change the embarrassing obscurity of Yunnan ethnic classics by making them known to the world, many of them for the first time.

In light of disciplinary development, the project is of great importance, too. Participating in the translation will strengthen the academic foundation of the teachers, enrich their experience and enhance their translation skills and research ability. This in turn will help them become better teachers and thus able to educate students with higher quality. The publication of the books will add greatly to the faculty accomplishments of the School and raise the academic standing of Yunnan Normal University by taking the first step in this direction among the universities of Yunnan province.

This publication project is a great event not only for Yunnan itself, but also for China. Looking back, I remember that Professor Li Changyin, our friend Li Lin, editor of the *Library of Chinese Classics*, and I talked enthusiastically about initiating something like this in Yunnan when we attended a conference on the translation of ethnic classics in Soochow. Lin and I strongly suggested that Professor Li do it as soon as possible. Now I am very pleased to see our talk becoming reality. Again, my congratulations on the publication of *Classics of Yunnan Ethnic Groups in English Translation*!

(Wang Hong, Vice Chairman of Classics Translation Committee of CACSEC, PhD supervisor at Soochow University)

导　言

　　"云南少数民族经典作品英译文库"旨在将云南少数民族的经典作品翻译介绍给国外对其感兴趣的英文读者大众。随着以古代汉文经典构成的"大中华文库"的出版发行，学界正将注意力转移到民族典籍的翻译上来。民族典籍是指由民族作家创作的反应民族历史和文化的经典作品。广西、贵州、辽宁、新疆、西藏等省区的大学已经捷足先登。我们云南也理应有所作为。云南拥有全国最多的少数民族。全省25个少数民族中，有15个为云南特有民族，即阿昌族、白族、布朗族、傣族、德昂族、独龙族、哈尼族、景颇族、基诺族、拉祜族、傈僳族、纳西族、怒族、普米族、佤族。这些民族的典籍，有的是原作，有的是汉译本，构成了一个巨大的宝库，我们有义务将其介绍给国外的英语读者和学术界。问题是，先译什么？

　　云南所有的25个少数民族都创造了自己的经典作品，包括史诗、神话、创世故事、民谣、戏曲、山歌和丧歌，以各种形式流传于各地，总数不下10万卷，这还不包括口传文体。经过调查研究，并征求民族学专家的建议后，我们决定重点翻译史诗和神话。史诗和神话叙述的是民族起源故事，最能反映各民族哲学、历史、文化等的概貌、渊源。我们从汗牛充栋的民族史诗与神话中精选了云南阿昌族、白族、傣族、德昂族、哈尼族、景颇族、拉祜族、苗族、纳西族、普米族、彝族等 11 个少数民族的 17 部最具有代表性的经典作品。这些作品全部都是汉语译本，由既会讲母语又精通汉语的双语学者整理、翻译而成。其中有的是在节庆仪式和表演时从口语录制而来。我们没有选择用民族语言写成的文本，首先是因为很难寻找到民族语和英语俱佳的译者；其次是因为一部分典籍的民族语言文本在民间以多种方言形式流传，情节五花八门。汉语文本系专家仔细整理、翻译而成，因而更具权威性。接下来的问题是：如何译？

在我们选定的 17 部作品中，除了《白国因由》为散文体之外，其余全部为民歌韵文体，诗行长度大致相当，行末有松散押韵，无格律。译诗为诗是最起码的要求。我们遵循的原则有如下几点。

一、若原文为诗歌，译文也必须为诗歌。

二、译文尽可能完整地再现原文的思想内容和意象。

三、译文尽可能再现原文的修辞手段。

四、不改变原文每一节诗的行数，除非万不得已。

五、不使用英文的标准格律，因为原文并不是标准的格律体。采用英文的自然节奏，但诗行长短应大体一致。

六、不用韵，除非符合英文表达习惯且不损害原文内容。

我们所追求的，用苏珊·巴斯奈特的话来说就是"异地播种"，而不是直接移栽树木。关于原文的形式特征，尤其是尾韵，能再现时再现，不能再现时果断放弃。

那谁来翻译呢？本文库是云南师范大学外国语学院的集体项目，因此我们的翻译团队由本院十几位同行加上两位在职攻读翻译专业硕士学位的高校教师组成。所有译者都在高校教授翻译课程，从事翻译研究，不仅发表了翻译论文，也出版了译著。

  传统上，人们通常是将外语译为母语，而不是将母语译为外语。但是这种情况正在发生改变。现在许多译者都将母语译为外语。根据耐克·帕科恩[①]和斯图亚特·坎贝尔[②]的论证，将母语译入非母语，能够达到相当高的水平。中国的情形为他们的观点提供了新的论据。中国典籍英译在19世纪由英国汉学家理雅各和翟理斯发起，20世纪在亚瑟·伟利、戴维·霍克思、波顿·沃森、约翰·闵福德、宇文所安等英美汉学家的推动下继续发展。值得注意的是，在这一过程中，旅居西方的华人学者迅速加入到了中国典籍英译的行列中。其中最著名的是辜鸿铭和林语堂。他们主动承担这个任务，因为他们认为西方汉学家的母语并非汉语，其译文往往误读汉语原文本，误解中国文化，自己义不容辞，必须为英语读者提供更忠实的英文翻译。自20世纪50年代开始，越来越多的中国大陆译者投身于典籍英译或重译。在杨宪益、许渊冲、汪榕培、王宏印、王宏、李正栓等当代翻译家和翻译理论家的积极倡导和引领下，典籍英译蔚然成风，势头强劲。许渊冲、王宏、李正栓等都在西方出版社出版了英文译著，这表明他们的英文水平达到了国际上的出版标准。

  就本文库而言，我们采取了一系列保障译文质量的措施。我们要求译者尽最大努力拿出代表自己最高水平的译文。文

---

① 挑战公理：译入非母语. 阿姆斯特丹：约翰·本杰明斯出版公司，2005.
② 译入第二语言. 纽约：劳特里奇出版社，2013.

库的主编们对译文进行仔细研读，纠正理解偏差、语法错误以及格式上的问题。在此基础上，我们采取了一个不可或缺的步骤，请长期在我院从事英语教学工作的美国老师包琼（Joan Cecile Boulerice）对每一个译本进行逐字逐句的修改，使之更自然流畅，更符合英文表达习惯。我们尽了最大的努力。如果译文还存在什么问题，皆由我们负责，与包琼老师无关。

在这里，我们对所有给予我们宝贵帮助和支持的专家学者深表谢忱。感谢云南人民出版社的领导为文库成功申报为"十三五"国家重点出版物出版规划项目和国家出版基金项目给予的大力支持。感谢文库责编、东南亚南亚读物编辑部主任郭木玉，她的严谨和敬业令我们动容。感谢云南师范大学为文库提供了出版资金支持，使译者们不被"眼前的苟且"干扰，能够一心一意地追求"诗和远方"。感谢李正栓教授和王宏教授不仅一直鼓励我们前进，而且欣然为文库作序，从全球视野对其意义进行肯定，极大地提振了我们的信心。感谢包琼老师，她的修改保证了译文的流畅性。最后要特别感谢王宏教授和湖南人民出版社的资深编辑李林先生，是他们的建议促成了本文库的构想。

云南师范大学外国语学院
"云南少数民族经典作品英译文库"编委会

General Introduction

This publication project, *Classics of Yunnan Ethnic Groups in English Translation*, aims at introducing Yunnan ethnic classical works to the world by making them available to native speakers of English who might be interested in them. With the publication of the *Library of Chinese Classics*, which consists only of books written by Han authors in classical Chinese, attention now is being turned to the English translation and publication of ethnic classics, books produced by ethnic writers about their history and culture. Universities in provinces such as Guangxi, Guizhou, Liaoning, Xinjiang, and Xizang, have taken the initiative. We in Yunnan must do something, because Yunnan has the largest number of ethnic groups in China. 15 of the 25 ethnic groups in the province, the Achang, the Bai, the Bulang, the Dai, the De'ang, the Dulong, the Hani, the Jingpo, the Jinuo, the Lahu, the Lisu, the Naxi, the Nu, the Pumi, and the Wa, live in no other place but Yunnan. The classics of these people, either in their own language or in Chinese translations, are a great treasure house, which should be accessible to English readers and scholars. But what works should be translated first?

All the 25 ethnic groups in Yunnan have their classics,

黑白之战 // The War Between the Black and the White Tribes

epics, mythology, creation stories, folksongs, folk drama, mountain songs, and funeral lament lyrics, most of which exist in different versions in different places. According to one estimation, there are more than 100,000 volumes of them, excluding those in oral form. After a thorough survey and extensive consultations with experts of ethnic studies, we concluded that priority must be given to epics and mythologies, as they reflect an ethnic people's philosophy, history and culture more than anything else by narrating the stories of where and how they think they came from. From many epics and mythologies, we selected 17 of the most authoritative and popular classics representing 11 Yunnan ethnic groups, the Achang, the Bai, the Dai, the De'ang, the Hani, the Jingpo, the Lahu, the Miao, the Naxi, the Pumi, and the Yi. These works are all in Chinese, translated from the original by bilingual scholars whose mother tongue is their own ethnic language and who are fluent and proficient in Chinese. Some were recorded from their oral form at rituals and performances. We did not choose texts written in the ethnic language, not least because it is very hard to find a translator who is skilled in both the ethnic language and English. Moreover, some of the classics in the ethnic language were circulated in various oral forms and fragments. The published Chinese versions have been carefully edited and translated, hence they are more reliable. The next question is: how to translate them?

It happens that all of the 17 works except one are in verse form, with lines more or less the same length and loose rhymes, but no regular meter. A poem must be rendered into a poem; anything less is unacceptable. So here are the general rules we follow when doing the translation.

One. If the original is verse, the translated text must be verse, too.

Two. Reproduce the ideas and the images of the original as completely as possible.

Three. Reproduce the figures of speech of the original as much as possible.

Four. Do not change the number of lines in a stanza unless absolutely necessary.

Five. Do not use standard meters in English, because the Chinese original does not follow any regular meter. Use the natural rhythm of English instead, but most of the lines should look more or less the same length.

Six. Do not use rhyme unless it comes naturally and is faithful to the content of the original.

What we try to do is, to use Susan Bassnett's words, "transplant the seed", not the tree itself. As for the various aspects of form, particularly meter and end rhyme, we reproduce them when it is possible and abandon them when it is necessary.

Who will do the translations? As this is a collective project of the School of Foreign Languages and Literature of Yunnan Normal University, our team consists of a dozen faculty members and two students from our MA translation program who are already teachers in other universities. All the translators have been teaching translation and doing translation research for a long time. They have published not just academic articles on translation, but also translated books from English to Chinese or vice versa.

Traditionally, people translate into their mother tongue, not into a foreign language. But the situation is changing. Many translators today are translating from their mother tongue into a foreign language. The quality can be good, as Nike K. Pokorn and Stuart Campbell prove in *Challenging the Traditional Axioms: Translation into a non-mother tongue* (Amsterdam: John Benjamins Publishing Company, 2005) and *Translation into the Second Language* (New York: Routledge, 2013) respectively. The case of China provides further evidence for their argument. The translation of Chinese classics into English was initiated by James Legge and Herbert Allen Giles in the 19th century and carried on in the 20th century by Arthur Waley, David Hawkes, Burton Watson, John Minford, Stephen Owen and others. It is noticeable that these English and American sinologists were soon joined by Chinese scholars residing in the West, such as Hongming (Tomson) Gu and Lin Yutang, among others. They took up the job because they thought it was their obligation to give English readers more faithful translations than Western sinologists could, who, as their target language is their mother tongue, often misinterpret the original text and misrepresent Chinese culture. Since the 1950s, there has been an increasingly powerful trend for Mainland Chinese translators to render or re-render Chinese classics into foreign languages, English in particular. In our time, this work is gathering momentum, enthusiastically advocated and actively practiced by such well-known translation experts as Yang Xianyi of Beijing Foreign Language Press, Xu Yuanchong of Beijing University, Wang Rongpei of Dalian Foreign Language Institute, Wang Hongyin of Nankai University, Wang Hong of Soochow University, Li Zhengshuan of Hebei Normal University, and many more. These professors are not just translators, but also scholars in translation studies. More importantly, some of them, Xu Yuanchong, Wang Hong and Li Zhengshuan, for example, have had their translations published by Western publishers, which suggests that their English meets the international standard.

In the case of our project, we request that the translators do their best to produce good translations. When they submit them to us, they should represent the highest level that they can attain. Then the general editors appointed by the School read the translated texts and remove inaccurate renderings and grammar mistakes if there are any. On top of that, we've taken an indispensable measure to ensure that our English is readable. We asked Ms. Joan Cecile Boulerice, an American teacher who has been teaching English in our school since 2009, to read every text that we've translated and improve the English by making it more natural and idiomatic. This is the best we can do. Of course any problems that still remain in the translations are ours. They have nothing to do with our American teacher.

As the project is well under way, we would like to thank all those who have helped to make it possible. Ms. Guo Muyu, director of the South and Southeast Asia Editorial Department, Yunnan People's Publishing House, has been most helpful in our cooperation. In addition, she has added importance to the project by turning it into a national publication project. Yunnan Normal University has supported us by paying the publication fees so that the translators won't have to be burdened with the financial responsibilities for this project. Professor Li Zhengshuan and Professor Wang Hong not only have always encouraged us to go on but have also written the forewords for the project, putting it in a global perspective. Ms. Joan Cecile Boulerice's revision has ensured the fluency of the translated texts. Finally, special thanks must be given to Professor Wang Hong, again, and Mr. Li Lin of Hunan People's Press for their suggestion that has helped us conceive the project from the very beginning.

The General Editors
School of Foreign Languages & Literature
Yunnan Normal University, Kunming

黑白之战 / 目录

天地初始 // 1

争战起源 // 9

术主行盗 // 19

日月重归 // 29

术子用计 // 39

米委丧生 // 55

乌鸦挑唆 // 65

术主寻衅 // 77

遣兵侦察 // 87

初战白海 // 103

耿饶茨嫫 // 113

阿璐上钩 // 129

身陷魔窟 // 147

黑白之战

目 录

术兵犯境 // 165

宁死不屈 // 183

茨嫫忏悔 // 201

东主返世 // 215

祖孙相逢 // 225

东术决战 // 237

光明永存 // 265

译后记 // 276

Contents

The Beginning of the World // 1

The Brewing of the War // 9

The Theft by Lord Shu // 19

The Restoring of the sun and the moon // 29

The Trick of Miwei // 39

The Death of Miwei // 55

The Incitement of the Raven // 65

The Provoking of Lord Shu // 77

The Spying of the Situation // 87

The Lakeside Fighting // 103

The Lure of Cimo // 113

The Hooking of Ahlu // 129

The Trapping of Ahlu // 147

The War Between the Black and the White Tribes / Contents

The Invasion of Shu's Soldiers // 165

The Unyielding of Ahlu // 183

The Remorse of Cimo // 201

The Return of Lord Dong // 215

The Reunion of Lord Dong's Family // 225

The Decisive Battle // 237

The Eternity of Light // 265

Translators' Afterword // 278

天地初始

The Beginning of the World

黑白之战 // The War Between the Black and the White Tribes

千古万古前，
没有地和天，
没有日月星，
没有海和山。

妙音出上方，
瑞气出下方；
音和气相合，
刮起白风来。

三股白风吹，
化为白云彩；
白云酿露浆，
白露凝白蛋。

白蛋孵开来，
五神[①]出世来，
东主[②]出世来，
术主[③]出世来。

[①] 五神：名盘、禅、高、吾、恒。
[②] 东主：善神米利东主。
[③] 术主：黑界米利术主。

天地初始
The Beginning of the World

Thousands upon thousands of years ago,
Neither the earth nor the sky came to light,
Nor were the sun, the moon and other stars,
Nor the lakes and the hills ever in sight.

Drifting from above were melodious notes,
Rising from below were lucky vapors;
When the notes and vapors came together,
Gentle breezes were puffed out in the sky.

Three of the breezes kept on blowing there,
With milky clouds resulting from the puffs;
The clouds then gave birth to some syrup,
Which in turn froze into some snowy eggs.

When the eggs got hatched thereafter,
Five divinities[①] were thus borne out,
Together with Lord Dong[②] the Righteous
And Lord Shu[③] his rival as the tale goes.

---

① Five divinities refer to Pan, Chan, Gao, Wu and Heng in Naxi folklore.
② In Naxi folklore Dong is the Lord of Light, whose full name is the Lord of Mili Dong.
③ In Naxi folklore Shu is the Lord of Dark, whose full name is the Lord of Mili Shu.

黑白之战 // The War Between the Black and the White Tribes

有了白天地，
有了白山川，
有了白风雨，
有了白牛羊；

有了黑天地，
有了黑山川，
有了黑风雨，
有了黑牛羊；

有了红天地，
有了红山川，
有了红风雨，
有了红牛羊；

有了黄天地，
有了黄山川，
有了黄风雨，
有了黄牛羊；

有了绿天地，
有了绿山川，

天地初始
The Beginning of the World

From this came the whitish skies and lands,
From this came the whitish hills and rivers,
From this came the whitish winds and rain,
From this came the whitish cattle and sheep;

From this came the blackish skies and lands,
From this came the blackish hills and rivers,
From this came the blackish winds and rain,
From this came the blackish cattle and sheep;

From this came the reddish skies and lands,
From this came the reddish hills and rivers,
From this came the reddish winds and rain,
From this came the reddish cattle and sheep;

From this came the yellowish skies and lands,
From this came the yellowish hills and rivers,
From this came the yellowish winds and rain,
From this came the yellowish cattle and sheep;

From this came the greenish skies and lands,
From this came the greenish hills and rivers,

有了绿风雨,
有了绿牛羊。

居那若倮山,
神山撑天地;
赠争含鲁石,
神石镇妖孽。

三朵白云彩,
再酿白露浆;
白露有一滴,
化为达吉海。

山有山生物,
海有海生物,
万类在繁衍,
万物在繁昌。

天地初始
The Beginning of the World

From this came the greenish winds and rain,
From this came the greenish cattle and sheep.

Juna Ruoluo stood forbiddingly high,
Propping up the sky as a huge mountain;
Zengzheng Hanlu crouched upon the earth,
Subduing monsters as a boulder blunt.

While three milky clouds were floating apart,
More dew drops were brewed like glue butter;
A cute drop falling off from the white dew,
Became a lake known by the name of Daji.

Alpine plants kept growing on the high hills,
Marine life kept thriving in the large lake,
Creatures were multiplied in great numbers,
So the forms of life were increased at a fast speed.

争战起源
The Brewing of the War

黑白之战 // The War Between the Black and the White Tribes

米丽达吉海,
海宽连云天,
海水如玉液,
海浪似金毯。

海心长神树,
幼苗细又软,
像根头发辫,
来回飘浪间。

恶鬼要砍树,
天神不许砍;
天神吼一声,
恶鬼吓破胆。

术主要伤苗,
东主来阻挡;
斯族要伤苗,
哈族来护防。

争战起源
The Brewing of the War

Well known by the full name Mili Daji,

The lake surges far and wide to the sky.

With its water much sweeter than nectar,

Its ripples glitter like a golden carpet.

In the middle of the lake grows a holy tree,

Whose seedling is slim, soft and tender.

Looking like a pigtail of black hair,

The tree keeps on waving back and forth.

Some monsters want to cut the holy tree,

Which is not allowed by the Divine.

A yell roared out by the great Divine,

Frightens off the heads of the monsters.

Lord Shu wants to harm the magic tree,

While Lord Dong is resolved to stop him.

The Si Tribe comes to hurt the seedling,

But the Ha Tribe comes to protect it.

黑白之战 // The War Between the Black and the White Tribes

恶鬼半夜来，
约着术族来，
约着斯族来，
偷偷把树砍。

天神领东族，
天神带哈族，
点下如意药，
断口重接好。

一天长三次，
一夜粗三次，
含英宝达树，
长成摩天树。

树分十二枝，
生出十二属；
枝生十二叶，
分出十二月。

叶是绸缎叶，
花是金银花；

争战起源
The Brewing of the War

The monsters come to do harm at midnight,

Accompanied by men from the Shu Tribe;

With help from warriors of the Si Tribe,

They cut down the tree in a sneaky way.

Leading some warriors from the Dong Tribe,

And fighters from the Ha Tribe as well,

The Divine applies a drop of medicine,

To the wound for a quick recovery.

For three times the tree grows in the daytime,

For three times the tree grows in the nighttime;

Caressed with loving care and nutrients,

The tree grows up to a towering height.

Twelve branches grow out from the trunk,

Each standing for a zodiac figure;

Twelve leaves spring out on every branch,

Each denoting a month of the year.

The leaves are of soft silk and satin,

While the flowers are of gold and silver;

黑白之战 // The War Between the Black and the White Tribes

珍珠结成串,
宝果压枝桠。
见了金银花,
见了珠宝果,
术与东争夺,
从此兴干戈。

大拉久主海,
海在若倮山,
碧玉铺成浪,
黄金砌作岸。

一对金鲤鱼,
摆尾游起来。
吸水又吐水,
含着金蛋玩。

看鱼嘴开合,
饮水有了谱;
看鱼吞金蛋,
吃饭有了谱。

鱼要活命水,

争战起源
The Brewing of the War

The heavy fruit forms strings of pearls,
Bending the branches.
Lured by the gold and silver flowers,
And attracted by the fine fruit of pearls,
Shu and Dong vie for its ownership,
And an apple of discord is thus sowed.

Another lake named Dala Jiuzhu
Is located at the foot of Mount Ruoluo.
Its waves are made of deep green jade,
And its banks are built of sparkling gold.

In the lake live a pair of goldfish,
Who learn to swim by wriggling their tails.
Drinking in and spitting out water,
Each plays with a gold ball in her mouth.

Watching the fish open and shut their mouths,
People learn to value their water resources;
Watching the fish swallow their gold balls,
People learn to appreciate their foodstuff.

Just as water means life to the fish,

黑白之战 // The War Between the Black and the White Tribes

人要吃穿戴；
术与东争抢，
从此动刀剑。
只待火星闪，
干柴就要燃；
只等引线动，
弩弓就要开。

平安人世间，
战云纷纷翻：
角与角相抵，
蹄与蹄相踩。

争战起源
The Brewing of the War

Food and clothes are basic human needs;
To claim basic needs vital for their tribes,
Shu and Dong are ready to fight a war.
So long as the embers come alive,
Fires are bound to flare up from dry wood;
So long as the bowstrings are pulled back,
The arrows are prepared for shooting.

In a world where peace used to prevail,
Dark clouds sweep across the sullen sky.
Horns become good weapons for fighting,
And hoofs function as tools for trampling.

术主行盗
The Theft by Lord Shu

黑白之战 // The War Between the Black and the White Tribes

若倮神山高,
耸入九重天。
太阳从左旋,
月亮往右转。

绕行三十天,
相见在山顶。
一月三十天,
古谱在这里。

神山分两半,
神山有两界。
界东日月明,
界西似夜晚。

神裔米利东,
住在山东面。
九座白石屋,
白得像银墙。

脚踏白的地,

术主行盗
The Theft by Lord Shu

Ruoluo the sacred mountain stands high,

Scraping the ninth layer of the sky.

To the left the sun keeps revolving;

To the right the moon keeps rotating.

Between each interval of thirty days,

They meet at the top of the mountain.

As for the number of days in a month,

This is the point where people trace to.

The mountain is divided into two parts,

With either forming a world of its own.

The eastern part is ablaze with light,

While the western one is as dark as night.

Being a descendent of the Divine,

Mili Dong lives on the eastern part.

His nine mansions are made of white stones,

And his palace walls are silvery white.

His people step upon the ground white,

黑白之战 // The War Between the Black and the White Tribes

头顶白的天；
太阳明晃晃，
月亮亮闪闪。

黑魔米利术，
住在山西面。
九座黑石屋，
黑得像焦炭。

脚踩黑的地，
冠戴黑的天；
黑风呜呜吼，
黑云浑茫茫。

尖峰隔两界，
树木不相缠；
黑白截然分，
飞鸟不往来。

东主有银鼠，
打洞日夜忙。
埋头方向偏，
打穿若倮山。

术主行盗
The Theft by Lord Shu

With the sky above always clean and bright.

The sun keeps shining in the daytime,

And the moon is blinking in the nighttime.

Mili Shu, as the rival of Lord Dong,

Lives on the western side of the mountain.

His nine mansions are made of black stones,

And his palace walls is charcoal black.

His people stand upon the ground dark,

With the sky above always dim and black.

Grimy winds roar and swirl around,

And dark clouds roll up blunt and blurring.

A peak protrudes as the dividing line,

Where vines and plants never intertwine.

The Black and the White are tribes in contrast,

Even their birds never fly side by side.

Among Dong's subjects is the Ermine,

Who busies himself digging a tunnel through Mount Ruoluo.

Since he starts in a wrong direction,

His tunnel goes mistakenly through.

黑白之战 // The War Between the Black and the White Tribes

洞口连白界，

洞尾通黑界。

金光漏出去，

银光漏出去。

金光有一束，

照亮术的山；

银光有一道，

照进术的房。

术主见金光，

睁眼像铜钵；

术主见银光，

张口不会合。

东地有太阳，

术主早垂涎；

东地悬月亮，

术心冒醋酸。

要把光明掳，

忙叫黑猪来：

术主行盗
The Theft by Lord Shu

The entrance is connected with the White,
While the exit leads right to the Black.
Then golden light shines through the tunnel,
And silvery light also shines through it.

A shaft of golden light from the White,
Lights up the mountain slope on Shu's side;
A shaft of silvery light from the White,
Pours into Shu's pitch-dark sitting room.

When Lord Shu catches the golden sun light,
He opens his eyes wide like bronze bowls;
When Lord Shu sees the silvery moonlight,
He forgets to close his opened mouth.

As for the sun shining in Dong's sky,
Shu has stayed covetous for a long time;
As for the moon hanging in Dong's sky,
He has remained envious for years.

In order to captivate the bright light,
Lord Shu mobilizes the Boar for help:

黑白之战 // The War Between the Black and the White Tribes

洞子再拱大，
洞口再拱宽。

挑水想搬井，
偷柴想背山。
贪口不解馋，
术主怀鬼胎。

遣贼去东界，
偷下金太阳，
窃下银月亮，
钻洞往回搬。

黑铁打铁链，
粗链拴太阳；
拴在铁柱上，
铁柱迸火光。

黑铜打铜链，
粗链拴月亮；
拴在铜柱上，
铜柱凝白霜。

术主行盗
The Theft by Lord Shu

The tunnel has to be enlarged still,
And the exit has to be widened still.

Longing for an unearned easy life,
Shu yearns for easy water and grain.
With none of his avarice quenched,
He begins to conceive an evil plot.

A thief sent by Lord Shu to Dong's land,
Picks up both the golden sun and the silvery moon;
Getting them wrapped up in a package,
He has them taken back through the tunnel.

A chain forged with iron by Shu's men,
Is used to bind the golden sun;
When the sun gets chained to an iron bar,
Sparks keep bursting off the iron bar.

A chain forged with brass by Shu's men,
Is used to bind the silvery moon;
When the moon gets chained to a brass bar,
White frost appears along the brass bar.

日月重归
The Restoring of the sun and the moon

黑白之战 // The War Between the Black and the White Tribes

太阳丢失了,
月亮遗落了,
光明不见了,
东主发慌了。

抬头望术界,
白光冲上天。
猜是术主偷,
想是术家抬。

池里黄金蛙,
胆大如猛象,
心细如猎犬,
派去当侦探。

银鼠错打洞,
一日悔三回;
听蛙要出行,
找东来求情:

"愿做金蛙伴,

日月重归
The Restoring of the sun and the moon

Hearing the news of the solar theft,

Hearing the news of the lunar theft,

And thinking of the loss of the light,

Lord Dong gets panicked and flustered.

Raising his head to look at Shu's sky,

Lord Dong catches a flash beaming upward;

Making a guess at the burglary,

He ascribes it to Shu for envy.

The golden Frog living in the pond

Is just as brave as an elephant;

Being as alert and cautious as a hound,

He is sent away to do spying work.

For his fault in digging the wrong hole,

The Ermine laments three times a day;

Hearing the proposal from the Frog,

He comes to Lord Dong for an assignment.

"To keep the golden Frog's company,

黑白之战 // The War Between the Black and the White Tribes

愿去当侦探。
赎过要立功,
敢去踏火焰。"

金蛙和银鼠,
边走边商量。
半夜鸡叫前,
来到术地方。

术主做好梦,
鼾声呼呼响。
三绺黑头发,
沿床垂下来。

银鼠银牙尖,
好像一把剪。
上去咬头发,
三绺齐咬开。

清早术起床,
舀水来洗脸;
梳头头发断,
气得手打战。

日月重归
The Restoring of the sun and the moon

I wish to serve as a detective;

To make up for my silly mistake,

I am ready to go through any big fire."

Having made a sound plan for the task,

The two friends are walking to Shu's land;

By the time the roosters crow at midnight,

They have snuck onto their foe's land.

Lord Shu is then having a fond dream,

With his snoring heard both far and near;

In his sleep three strands of his black hair,

Fall straight over the edge of his bed.

When the Ermine catches sight of the strands,

He gnashes his teeth like sharp scissors;

Dashing forward for an angry bite,

He cuts off the hair strands all at once.

When Lord Shu gets up the next morning,

He washes his face with clean water;

But his hair comes off at his combing,

And his hands shake and tremble in anger.

黑白之战 // The War Between the Black and the White Tribes

黑鼠蹲柱旁,
鼠牙像针尖。
术猜是它咬,
怒火烧牙关。

拣根粗棍子,
掐住鼠脖子,
打翻在地上,
踩扁在地上。

蠢汉做蠢事,
铁柱无人守。
金蛙和银鼠,
偷偷笑不休。

金蛙去巡风,
银鼠奔上前,
咬断粗铁索,
放开金太阳。

金蛙守窗户,
银鼠奔铜柱。

日月重归
The Restoring of the sun and the moon

The black Mouse crouches beside a pillar,

Exposing his teeth as sharp as needles.

Believing him to be the trickster,

Lord Shu gnashes his teeth in great despair.

Snatching up a rough club in his hand,

Lord Shu seizes the Mouse by the neck in rage;

Throwing the Mouse down onto the ground,

He stamps on him with his huge foot.

Due to Lord Shu's reckless silly actions,

No one is assigned to watch the bar.

When the Frog and Ermine see that chance,

They have a good laugh behind themselves.

With the golden Frog standing sentry,

The Ermine dashes toward one pillar;

Biting the tough cable with all his might,

He tries to set the fettered sun free.

With the Frog watching at the window,

The Ermine rushes toward the other pillar;

黑白之战 // The War Between the Black and the White Tribes

咬断粗铜链,
放开银月亮。

银鼠扛月亮,
金蛙驮太阳,
嘻嘻哈哈笑,
赶回东地来。

东手挂月亮,
东掌托太阳,
秘咒念三遭,
谁也偷不了。

黑暗还术地,
术界黑漆漆;
光明回东境,
东地亮晶晶。

日月重归
The Restoring of the sun and the moon

Gnawing at the cable with all his might,
He tries to set the fettered moon free.

The Ermine takes the moon on his shoulder,
While the Frog carries the sun on his back;
Cracking jokes and laughing all the way,
They return to their homeland in triumph.

With pleasure Lord Dong hangs the recovered moon,
With delight Lord Dong hangs the recovered sun;
Three times he repeats some charms and spells,
So as to have them kept safe and sound.

When the dark rays come back to Shu's land,
Black clouds hover as they did before;
When bright rays come back to Dong's land,
White clouds prevail as they did before.

术子用计
The Trick of Miwei

黑白之战 // The War Between the Black and the White Tribes

米利东主呵,
爱儿有九个;
茨爪金嫫呵,
爱女有九个。

巴掌分五指,
不会一般齐;
九男和九女,
巧拙两分明。

美男名阿璐,
直树无疙瘩。
好像沙里金,
好像草里花。

好汉是阿璐,
能手夺天巧。
金嫫惜如珠,
东主爱如宝。

骏马蹄生风,

术子用计
The Trick of Miwei

Oh, his highness of Lord Mili Dong,

Is bestowed with nine courageous sons;

Alas, her highness Cizhua Jinmo,

Is blessed with nine beautiful daughters.

Although five fingers does a palm have,

They are no doubt of unequal length;

As for Dong's eighteen sons and daughters,

Some are smarter but the others slower.

As the most hunkiest among the guys,

Ahlu is a straight trunk without scars;

He is like gold glittering in the sand,

Or a red flower in the green grass.

As a worthy hero of great deeds,

Ahlu acquires good skills for fighting;

He is seen by his mom as a pearl,

And loved by his dad as a piece of jade.

A gallant steed with a fleet of foot,

黑白之战 // The War Between the Black and the White Tribes

早日架鞍子；
阿璐肩膀铁，
早日挑担子。

日月丢复得，
东主倍提防。
千斤交阿璐，
派去巡界边。

光明得又丢，
术主不甘心。
眉头皱成沟，
想起小儿子：

"安森米委呀，
心有七个窍；
像笛有七眼，
可吹百个调。

"好儿米委呀，
肠有九道弯；
像绳绕九曲，
捆宝靠你来！"

术子用计
The Trick of Miwei

Would be saddled at an early age;

An iron-shouldered man like Ahlu,

Would be entrusted with an early task.

Drawing lessons from the burglary,

Lord Dong becomes doubly vigilant;

Assigning his son with a great task,

He sends him to patrol the border.

Because of the light first gained then lost,

Lord Shu would never accept the defeat;

With his eyebrows knit in concentration,

He pictures the profile of his child:

"My dear youngest son Ansen Miwei,

Is indeed brilliant and resourceful;

Like a flute with seven holes aligned,

He can play a multitude of tones.

"Oh Miwei, my youngest darling son,

How cunning and shrewd you are indeed;

Like a rope winding along the creek,

You are competent to take the light back."

黑白之战 // The War Between the Black and the White Tribes

撵鹿狗有意,
遇狗鹿无心。
米委和阿璐,
碰头在边境。

米委拉阿璐,
铺下白披毡;
掏出白骰子,
两人掷起来。

渔人下香饵,
诱鱼上钩来。
米委故意输,
阿璐花了眼。

米委笑着问:
"东天多光彩,
东地万物长,
是谁造出来?"

阿璐夸海口:
"天地日月星,

术子用计
The Trick of Miwei

The hound chases after the deer on purpose,

While the deer bumps into him by chance;

The two handsome men, like hound and deer,

Meet at the borderline of their lands.

To invite Ahlu to a game of dice,

Miwei spreads a white felt over the ground;

Taking out the white dice,

The two men take turns throwing the dice.

Like fishermen using worms for bait,

Miwei uses the dice to lure Ahlu;

His pretended loss at the game of dice

Deprives Ahlu of his sound judgment.

Then Miwei asks Ahlu with a smile:

"How brilliant and lustrous your sky is!

And all the living things on your land,

Who brings them into being, my dear friend?"

Feeling haughty Ahlu makes a boast:

"The sky, the land, the sun, the moon and the other stars,

山川木石水,
都是我造的。"

鱼儿要上钩,
米委把饵添。
亲热像兄弟,
话里拌蜜糖:

"阿璐真能干,
阿璐赛神仙。
请来辟术地,
请来开术天。

"金银随你拿,
拿去用牛驮;
珠宝随你装,
装来用马驮。"

小鱼吞香饵,
不知钩刺藏:
"米委你放心,
隔天我就来。"

术子用计
The Trick of Miwei

And the mountains, the woods, the rocks, and the rivers,

Are all fine creations of my own hands."

When the bait is about to be taken,

A greater amount should be added;

Pretending to be a sworn brother,

Miwei utters in a honeyed tone:

"As a competent guy in the real sense,

You are more capable than a divine;

Would you please come to remold our land,

And rebuild our sky in the meantime?

"Take any treasure you wish in return,

Such as gold and silver on cattle backs;

Take whatever pearl or jewel as you like,

And pack and pile them upon horse backs."

The fish devours his delicious bait,

Unaware of the trick that lurks ahead;

"Please rest assured and relieved, my friend,

I'll come to your help two days later."

黑白之战 // The War Between the Black and the White Tribes

阿璐见父亲，
说要去术地。
东主忙摇头，
苦劝不让行：

"上山不提防，
魔鬼会来缠；
走路不小心，
脚会撞石块。

"狐狸不小心，
也会被虎咬；
男儿不听话，
会被仇人杀。"

阿璐见母亲，
说要去术地。
金嫫摆摆手，
拦住不准走：

"三道鬼旋涡，
旋在你头上；
一道凶花纹，

术子用计
The Trick of Miwei

When Ahlu goes to see his father,

He tells him he will go to Shu's land;

Shaking his head in a great hurry,

Lord Dong tries to persuade him not to go:

"Failing to look out when climbing hills,

You are sure to be haunted by devils;

Being careless while taking a walk,

You are destined to tumble over rocks.

"When a fox fails to watch out for himself,

He might be assaulted by a tiger;

When a man listens not to reason,

He might be killed by his enemy."

When Ahlu goes to see his mother,

He tells her he will go to Shu's land;

Waving her hand in a great hurry,

Jinmo tries to stop her son from going:

"I see three vortexes of ill omen,

Spiraled above the hair on your head;

I spot a pattern of bad fortune,

黑白之战 // The War Between the Black and the White Tribes

刻在你手上。

"三个短命记,
烙在你腰间。
你要去仇家,
我心真不安。"

父亲劝九遍,
阿璐不点头;
母亲劝七遍,
阿璐光摇头:

"吃肉不兴吐,
说话不兴悔。
盟约订在先,
不去丢脸皮。"

妈呵没办法,
嘱儿莫怠意;
爹呵劝不转,
授儿安身计:

"神鬼不一样,

术子用计
The Trick of Miwei

Engraved in the palm of your left hand.

"I find three tokens for a short life,

Vaguely inscribed upon your back;

If you insists on meeting your enemy,

How can I feel relieved about your trip?"

Though nine times his father talks to him,

Ahlu refuses to give any nod;

Though seven times his mom advises him,

Ahlu shakes his head in stubbornness:

"One must swallow the meat of his bite,

And keep the words that he has uttered;

Since my promise was made in advance,

What a shame it would be to break it!"

For this his mother could do nothing,

But beg him to be always alert;

Nor is his father able to stop him,

So he has to offer him useful tricks:

"Gods and monsters are not the same species,

黑白之战 // The War Between the Black and the White Tribes

东术不一般。
术地要斜辟,
术天要歪开。

"黑白不一样,
东术非睦邦。
术山要斜辟,
术川要歪开。

"夜深狗不吠,
快回交界边:
栽起铜棘来,
安起铁铡来!"

术子用计
The Trick of Miwei

Neither are the lords from the two tribes;

Be sure to chop Shu's land aslant,

And be sure to hack Shu's sky askew.

"Pursuing different values in life,

We two tribes are neighbors on bad terms;

Shu's mountains must be chopped aslant,

And his rivers must be dug askew.

"When the dogs become mute late at night,

Return to the border without delay;

Put up copper spikes for your defense,

And iron choppers as well for help!"

米委丧生
The Death of Miwei

黑白之战 // The War Between the Black and the White Tribes

阿璐到术家,
米委笑脸迎。
阿璐显身手,
米委献殷勤。

挥斧开术天,
开得歪歪的。
好像草锅盖,
歪盖在云里。

舞剑辟术地,
辟成斜斜的。
好像木楼梯,
斜架在屋顶。

术王赠金银,
翠玉盘子装;
米委送珠宝,
五色丝线拴。

蒙住阿璐心,

米委丧生
The Death of Miwei

When arriving in Shu's territory,

Ahlu is received by the smiling face of Miwei;

Given a chance to show his talent,

He enjoys the attention from Miwei.

When chopping at the sky with his axe,

He works on it as he was instructed;

Like the straw cover for a cauldron,

It covers the clouds in a slanting way.

When cutting out the land with his sword,

He works on it as he is instructed;

Like a slanting ladder made of wood,

It leans against the roof of Shu's sky.

To give Ahlu his silver and gold,

Shu uses his jade plate as a holder;

To present his jewelry to Ahlu,

Miwei has them bound with colored threads.

Faced with so much gold and jewelry,

黑白之战 // The War Between the Black and the White Tribes

迷了阿璐眼。
爹妈临行话，
忘在耳后边。

一睡合眼皮，
鼾声如雷鸣。
米委暗暗笑，
忙去偷光明。

半夜人声静，
有狗也不吠。
心宽忘百忧，
沉睡如酒醉。

梦见恶狗扑，
猛然被惊醒。
金宝揣三把，
如风溜回程。

米委过界东，
上前盗日月；
阿璐落界西，
在后设陷阱。

米委丧生
The Death of Miwei

Ahlu feels enchanted and bewildered;
The farewell advice from his parents,
Seems to have escaped from his mind.

With his eyelids closed while asleep,
Ahlu snores more loudly than thunders;
Tittering and snickering in his beard,
Miwei hurries to steal the sky lamps.

At night when all creatures are asleep,
The guardian dogs become as mute as fish;
With his mind freed of all nasty cares,
Ahlu falls fast asleep like a dead log.

Seeing an assaulting dog in his dream,
Ahlu becomes startled and wide awake;
With treasures stuffed in his pockets,
He flees to the border like the wind.

Crossing the border into Dong's land,
Miwei walks straight to the sun and the moon;
Having landed west of the borderline,
Ahlu sets traps for defense behind him.

黑白之战 // The War Between the Black and the White Tribes

东家穿山眼，
看见黑影闪。
黑手摘月亮，
月光乱摇晃。

东家顺风耳，
听见黑脚踩。
黑手扯太阳，
发出叮当响。

雷霆一声喊，
东兵追过来；
大风一声吼，
东将赶上来。

米委心发麻，
脚抖如跳蚤。
丢下日和月，
拼命往回逃。

铜棘勾双脚，
扑地嘴啃泥；

米委丧生
The Death of Miwei

General Pierce-Eye under Lord Dong,

Witnesses the flash of a black figure;

He sees a black hand grabbing at the moon,

While the moon keeps clanking and waving.

General Phone-Ear under Lord Dong,

Hears the tramping sound of the black feet;

He sees a black hand pulling at the sun,

While the sun keeps tinkling and jingling.

At the thundering yell from Lord Dong,

His brave warriors sweep along the way;

At the deafening shout like a gusting wind,

His generals keep surging like waves.

Miwei feels numb at the yell and shout,

And he dodges away like a scared flee;

Letting go off both the sun and the moon,

He runs for his life as fast as he can.

With both feet caught in the copper spikes,

Miwei falls to the ground on his face;

黑白之战 // The War Between the Black and the White Tribes

铁铡咔嚓响,
转眼命归阴。

千人围过来,
千声骂盗贼;
万人涌上来,
万嘴吐口水。

割下魔贼头,
来祭日月神。
血水洗刀刃,
界边来示警。

撬开九层土,
压着黑魔尸,
土上开水渠,
不让鬼翻身。

米委丧生
The Death of Miwei

At the cracking of the iron choppers,
He is sent to death in the blink of an eye.

Surrounding Miwei in a large circle,
Dong's soldiers curse the thief with bad words;
Pouring into the crowd for a look,
They spit onto the thief with scorn.

With the head of the burglar cut off,
They offer a sacrifice for the lamps;
Getting their knives washed in the blood,
They make the border a scene of warning.

Digging up nine layers of soil,
They bury the body deep below;
Building a ditch over the tomb mound,
They give the soul no chance for rebirth.

乌鸦挑唆
The Incitement of the Raven

黑白之战 // The War Between the Black and the White Tribes

九层白土上,
开凿白水渠。
金锄遍地挥,
银锄漫天舞。

东家狗獾子,
挖沟多卖力;
东家吸风鹰,
扒土不愿歇。

乌鸦贪游玩,
跳来又跳去,
怕苦怕沾灰,
不扒一把土。

哪里有火烟,
它往哪里瞧;
哪里有血肉,
它朝哪里跑。

毒刺生倒钩,

乌鸦挑唆
The Incitement of the Raven

Over the nine layers of white soil,

A white ditch is under construction;

Golden hoes are seen waving about,

Silvery hoes are seen wielding about.

The white Badger from Dong's family,

Behaves himself well digging the ditch;

The white Eagle from Dong's family,

Never stops pushing aside the soil.

But the playful Raven, nevertheless,

Keeps jumping back and forth all the time;

Fearing both hardships and sufferings,

He gives no hand to the digging of soil.

Wherever smoke rises over the site,

He stretches out his neck for a look;

Wherever bloody meat is served for food,

He dashes toward it for fear of being late.

As poisonous thorns are armed with barbs,

黑白之战 // The War Between the Black and the White Tribes

恶狗先咬人。
东主来沟边,
乌鸦挑是非:

"老鹰不开沟,
光朝火烟飞;
狗獾不扒土,
只往红肉奔。

"日出又日落,
挖土我最苦。
泥巴洗不赢,
腰弯像张弓。"

乌云遮青天,
东眼被遮住;
黑土埋金子,
东心被埋住。

东主骂老鹰,
不许来吃米。
老鹰吸凉风,
原因在这里。

乌鸦挑唆
The Incitement of the Raven

Vicious dogs are on guard against people;

And upon Lord Dong's arrival at the ditch,

The Raven makes up a false report:

"Grudging a helping hand to the work,

The Eagle flies only to smoke columns;

Unwilling to pull aside any soil,

The Badger cares only for red meat.

"Throughout the day from morning till night,

I work hardest in digging the earth;

To wash mud off my feet in the ditch,

I bend my waist like a pulled bow."

Like a blue sky shadowed by dark clouds,

Lord Dong's eyes are blinded by the false report;

Like real gold covered under black soil,

Lord Dong's mind gets blurred by the slander.

Putting an unfair scolding on the Eagle,

Lord Dong forbids him to eat any raw rice;

Now the eagle takes in cold air for food,

That's how he got into this habit.

黑白之战 // The War Between the Black and the White Tribes

东主骂狗獾,
不许来喝水。
狗用舌舔水,
原因在这里。

金蜂不服气,
银蝶抱不平。
跑到东身边,
争先诉真情:

"鹰在展劲扒,
狗在埋头挖。
乌鸦乱诬告,
偷懒正是它。"

沙沉水变清,
东主怒气升。
挥起金拐杖,
砸向乌鸦嘴。

乌鸦吓一跳,
急忙躲一旁。

乌鸦挑唆
The Incitement of the Raven

Placing an unfair scolding on the Badger,

Lord Dong forbids him to drink any water;

Now the badger drinks water by lapping,

That's how he got into this habit.

Feeling indignant at the slander,

The Wasp and the Butterfly take action;

Turning to Lord Dong for fair reports,

They are anxious to bring back the truth:

"The Eagle digs up the earth with great efforts,

And the Badger busies himself with his work;

But the Raven has made up a distorted report,

And it is him who loafs in the work."

When the true picture is discovered,

Lord Dong becomes angry and resentful;

Shaking and waving his walking stick,

He thrusts it at the beak of the Raven.

Being awfully scared and terrified,

The Raven dodges quickly to the side;

黑白之战 // The War Between the Black and the White Tribes

拍拍黑翅膀,
仓皇逃西方。

猫儿要偷鱼,
打死改不了;
乌鸦要饶舌,
百年变不了。

逃到术家来,
摆出可怜相。
翻动两面舌,
又把是非搬:

"你家好米委,
被东杀死了;
当作死老鼠,
埋进地狱了。

"土上开水渠,
水上撒麸糠。①
难道不气愤?

---

① 在纳西族传说中,在坟地上开渠、撒糠可以使鬼魂无法复生。

乌鸦挑唆
The Incitement of the Raven

Flapping and fluttering his black wings,

He flees westward in a great hurry.

The Cat likes to steal fish for food,

A habit till the end of his life;

The Raven is fond of making gossip,

A habit he sticks to forever.

Having arrived at Shu's family,

The Raven pretends to be innocent;

Making ill use of his eloquence,

He wishes to sow a seed of discord:

"What a bloody scene it is to witness,

The death of Miwei, your lovely son;

Disposed of and buried like a dead mouse,

In hell without any hope of rebirth.

"They then built a ditch over the soil,

And cast chaff over to stop his rebirth;[①]

Don't you feel wrathful and irritated?

---

① In Naxi legend, building channels and casting chaff over a tomb are used to prevent the soul from getting reborn.

黑白之战 // The War Between the Black and the White Tribes

难道不悲伤?

"东叫我开沟,
泥巴沾满脚;
一天挖到晚,
累得气要脱。

"不给我吃喝,
还要打死我。
好心的术主,
难道不怜我?

"麦子变毒草,
邻里变仇家。
有气能不出?
有仇能不报?

"蚯蚓没骨头,
怎能当蚯蚓?
雀子受鹰欺,
怎能当雀子?"

乌鸦挑唆
The Incitement of the Raven

Don't you feel bitter and resentful?

"At Lord Dong's order to dig the ditch,
My feet got stained with dirt and mud.
Digging hard from morning till evening,
I toiled almost to the end of my life.

"Giving me nothing to eat or drink,
He even threatened to beat me to death;
Your Highness, my benevolent master,
Won't you show me but a little mercy?

"As wheat may become poisonous weeds,
Neighbors may become hostile enemies;
Should you confine your anger to yourself?
Should you restrain yourself from revenge?

"Will you take whatever comes your way,
Like an earghworm bullied by other creatures?
Will you be a weak and meek sparrow,
Shamed and humiliated by the Eagle?"

术主寻衅
The Provoking of Lord Shu

黑白之战 // The War Between the Black and the White Tribes

母鸟失儿雏,
悲鸣鸣三天。
耿饶纳嫫呵,
痛哭哭连天。

火种借风燃,
风助火烧山。
乌鸦煽醋风,
术主捶胸膛:

"生儿生九个,
个个像猛虎,
不如米委勇,
米委是黑龙。

"生女生九个,
个个像凤凰,
不如米委好,
米委是只鸾。

"金鸡偷不来,

术主寻衅
The Provoking of Lord Shu

A mother bird may coo for three days,
Bemoaning the death of her dear child;
Gengrao Namo, mother of Miwei,
Cries her heart out for the loss of her son.

Kindled by the blowing of a strong wind,
The flames engulf the hill in violence;
Egged on and stirred by the vicious Raven,
Lord Shu beats his chest in great anguish.

"Altogether we have raised nine sons,
Each and every one like a fierce tiger;
But none is comparable with Miwei,
Who belongs to the species of dragon.

"In all we have nurtured nine daughters,
Each being prettier than a phoenix;
But none is comparable with Miwei,
Who is more gorgeous than the phoenix.

"First he only meant to go for wool,

黑白之战 // The War Between the Black and the White Tribes

倒反赔了米，
日月偷不来，
倒反赔了命。

"像割我头发，
像摘我心肝，
像砍我右臂，
像挖我左眼。

"鸢鸟自碰网，
东也太欺人。
闷气难下咽，
拼死战一回！"

术主与纳嫫，
深夜在密谈；
术主与大将，
清早在商量。

肯子丹由来，
那日左普来，
米麻生登来，[①]

[①] 三人均为术将。

术主寻衅
The Provoking of Lord Shu

But never thought of coming back shorn;

He only wished to get the lamps,

But never thought them to be fatal.

"His death is like the cutting of my hair,

Or the pulling out of my heart and liver,

Or the amputating of my right arm,

Or the digging out of my left eyeball.

"My fowl throws himself into the net,

But Dong has long been such a bully.

How can I take our ill fate lying down?

I'll fight against him till my last breath!"

Lord Shu and his wife Gengrao Namo

Are having a talk deep in the night;

Lord Shu and his army generals

Are making a plan in the morning.

Kenzi Danyou comes to stand muster,

Nari Zuopu comes to stand muster,

And Mima Shengdeng comes to stand muster, [①]

---

① These three men are Lord Shu's generals.

– 81 –

黑白之战 // The War Between the Black and the White Tribes

一起在筹商:

要带九千兵,
要选九百将,
报仇擒阿璐,
东族要杀光!

三山铁杉树,
砍下削长矛;
三谷藤与竹,
割来编铠甲。

长矛千千万,
锋利如铁锥;
铠甲万万千,
坚实像石墙。

铁匠来千个,
赶制铁盔帽;
火炉烧千个,
赶打长短刀。

犏牛杀千双,

术主寻衅
The Provoking of Lord Shu

Together they are conceiving a scheme:

Collecting nine thousand as soldiers,

Choosing nine hundred as commanders,

They vow to take revenge and catch Ahlu,

And kill all the people on Dong's land!

Cutting hemlocks from the bushy hills,

They make spears and shafts for their soldiers;

Cutting vines and bamboo from the valleys,

They make strong armor for their fighters.

The spears and shafts made of hemlock,

Serve as daggers for the brave soldiers;

The armor made of the vines and bamboos,

Serve as stone walls for the brave soldiers.

Gathering one thousand good blacksmiths,

They make strong helmets for their soldiers;

Making fires in one thousand large ovens,

They forge machetes for their brave army.

Killing one thousand pairs of oxen,

黑白之战 // The War Between the Black and the White Tribes

牦牛杀千双；
弯角做硬弓，
皮条做箭弦。

山雕斩一万，
山鸡杀一万；
羽毛插箭尾，
造出雕翎箭。

股股黑卷风，
刮过边界来。
刮倒白的树，
刮垮白的房。

支支黑羽箭，
射到东地来。
射落白的鸟，
射伤白的羊。

界石要崩了，
界水要决了，
火链击火石，
战火要烧了。

术主寻衅
The Provoking of Lord Shu

Plus one thousand pairs of fat yaks,

They produce bows with their curved horns,

And quality strings with fine ox-hides.

Killing ten thousand mountain eagles,

Plus ten thousand mountain pheasants,

They produce arrows for the fierce battle,

With feathers fixed at the end for balance.

Like dark hurricanes whirling around,

They cross the border for an attack;

Burning down trees near the boundary,

They loot all on their invading route.

Showers of arrows with black feathers,

Are heard whistling into the eastern land;

They kill flocks of birds flying in the sky,

And herds of sheep grazing in the fields.

Like the collapse of a heavy rock,

Or the overflow of a huge lake,

A fierce battle is doomed to break out,

When a flint is struck against the iron.

遣兵侦察
The Spying of the Situation

黑白之战 // The War Between the Black and the White Tribes

天阴要下雨,
蚂蚁早知道。
术要来侵扰,
东主早料到。

金蜂当探兵,
身轻耳目灵。
东主派金蜂,
术地探真情。

金黄小蜜蜂,
飞到黑屋顶。
术家马蜂恶,
一齐来包围。

术主来拷问,
金蜂紧闭嘴;
术主来劝诱,
金蜂不搭理。

硬审有九遍,

遣兵偵察
The Spying of the Situation

When dark clouds roll over in the sky,

A shower is often foretold by the ant;

When Shu plans to launch an invasion,

His plot is anticipated by Lord Dong.

The golden Bee, as a nimble spy,

Is armed with keen hearing and eyesight;

Sent by Lord Dong to the front as a scout,

He wishes to find out the real facts.

When the Bee reaches his destination,

He stops on the roof of the Shu's black house;

Seeing an assault of a swarm of wasps,

He finds himself tightly encircled.

When questioned by Lord Shu about his mission,

The creature simply closes his mouth;

When persuaded by Lord Shu to surrender,

He responds to him with mere silence.

After nine times of torture with rough sticks,

黑白之战 // The War Between the Black and the White Tribes

软劝有七回。
金蜂生怒气,
螫了术一针。

术主下毒手,
割下蜂舌头。
金蜂飞回来,
忍哩软啷嚷。

(蜜蜂飞千里,
忍哩软啷叫,
有话说不清,
原因在这里。)

鲤鱼当探兵,
身巧嘴伶俐。
东派金鲤鱼,
术地探实情。

金黄小鲤鱼,
游到黑屋底。
术家黑鱼狂,
群起来包围。

遣兵偵察
The Spying of the Situation

And seven times of coaxing with sweet words,

The Bee bursts into a huge rage and fury,

And gives Lord Shu a prompt hit with his stinger.

As the result of Lord Shu's merciless blow,

The Bee's tongue is cut off with a knife;

When he returns home without a tongue,

Buzzing is all he can do from then on.

(The bee can fly a long distance though,

Yet only buzzing sounds can he make;

He may wish to make himself clearer,

But the cause for his failure lies here.)

Being quick, nimble, and talkative as well,

The Carp is sent for detection, too;

Dispatched to the land under Shu's rule,

He wishes to collect data for the war.

When the Carp reaches his destination,

He stays at the bottom of Shu's house,

But finds himself closely encircled,

By a school of fish at Shu's order.

黑白之战 // The War Between the Black and the White Tribes

术主来拷问,
金鱼紧闭嘴。
术主来劝诱,
金鱼不搭理。

恶审有九遍,
甜劝有七回。
金鱼生忿心,
咬了术一嘴。

术主下毒手,
割掉鱼舌头。
金鱼转回程,
伸嘴又缩嘴。

(金鱼游水里,
嘴巴缩又伸,
有话说不成,
原因在这里。)

东主看在眼,
猫爪抓心坎。

遣兵偵察
The Spying of the Situation

When questioned by Lord Shu about his mission,

The creature simply closes his mouth;

When persuaded by Lord Shu to surrender,

He responds to him with mere silence.

After nine times of torture with rough sticks,

And seven times of coaxing with sweet words,

He bursts into a rage and fury,

And gives Lord Shu a prompt bite with his teeth.

As a result of Shu's merciless blow,

The Carp's tongue is cut off with a knife;

When he returns home without a tongue,

Bobbling is all he can do from then on.

(The carp can swim a long distance though,

Yet only babbling sounds can he make;

He may wish to make himself clearer,

But the cause for his failure lies here.)

When Lord Dong sees his Bee and Carp wounded,

He feels as if his heart were slashed;

黑白之战 // The War Between the Black and the White Tribes

又把白云派，
又将白风遣。

白风空中刮，
白云天上飘。
术地藏杀机，
一眼看透了。

白云飞下天，
向东来递信；
白风旋下天，
找东来报讯：

"术地铠甲多，
好像树叶飘；
术地刀矛多，
好像乱草草。

"铁盔像鹰群，
战马像蚂蚁，
长弓像蛇阵，
箭似蜜蜂飞。

遣兵侦察
The Spying of the Situation

Promptly he sends the Cloud as a spy,

Attended by the Wind in case of needing help.

The white Wind is blowing in the air,

And the white Cloud floating in the sky;

They see through the storm over Shu's land,

An evil plan for indiscriminate butchery.

Floating down from the sky to the ground,

The Cloud comes with a message to Lord Dong;

Swirling down from the sky to the ground,

The Wind brings his report back to Lord Dong:

"The armor assembled over Shu's land,

Look like piles of leaves fallen off trees;

The spears and knives gathered in Shu's land,

Look like haystacks stored for herds of cattle.

"The iron helmets look like flying eagles,

And the horses are like moving ant swarms;

The long bows look like winding snakes,

And the arrows form an army of bees.

黑白之战 // The War Between the Black and the White Tribes

"会飞的在飞,
会跳的在跳,
会砍的在砍,
会杀的在杀。

"罗堆古扭来,
立了三个寨;
罗霸季登来,
立了三个寨。

"六寨鬼怪兵,
昼夜在操演。
左普是箭官,
丹由是总管。

"呆兵像狐狸,
拉兵像虎狼,
毒兵像牛头,
仄兵像马面。

"蒙兵像水妖,
恩兵獠牙尖。
黑云滚滚起,

遣兵侦察
The Spying of the Situation

"Some eagles are hovering in the sky,

Some animals are tramping the ground,

Some enemies are killing with their knives,

And others are thrusting with their spears.

"There comes General Luodui Guniu,

To set up three stockades for his men;

There comes General Luoba Jideng,

To set up three stockades for his men.

"These monstrous soldiers from Shu's barracks,

Keep on training and drilling day and night;

Zuopu shows them ways for shooting arrows,

While Danyou cares for logistic affairs.

"The Dai squad of soldiers look like foxes,

The La squad of soldiers look like tigers,

The Du squad of soldiers look like oxen,

And the Ze squad look like strong horses.

"The Meng squad of soldiers look like demons,

And the En squad snarl their sharp teeth.

When clouds keep rolling over the ground,

黑白之战 // The War Between the Black and the White Tribes

天地暗无光。"①

东主听了笑，
暗笑黑魔疯：
鸡蛋碰石头，
飞蛾要扑火！

九座白山上，
白兵来布岗；
七条白谷里，
白兵来设防。

东兵站高山，
好像树满山；
东将进深谷，
好像大河淌。

阿璐像斑虎，
走路风呼呼。
斑虎下山来，
黑魔像灰鼠。

---
① 呆、拉、毒、仄、蒙、恩：均为术鬼之名。

遣兵侦察
The Spying of the Situation

Shu's land is shrouded in pitch-dark clouds."[1]

Hearing detailed reports from the front,
Lord Dong no longer holds back his contempt:
Shu is throwing his egg at a rock,
Or flying into the fire like a moth.

In the guardhouses built on nine hillocks,
Soldiers from the White Tribe stand guarding;
In the fortresses along seven valleys,
Soldiers from the White Tribe keep watching.

When Dong's soldiers line up on the slopes,
They resemble forests on the mountain;
When Dong's generals march in the valley,
They make up a huge river flowing.

Patrolling around his headquarters,
Ahlu walks like a howling tiger;
Seeing the tiger leaping off the hill,
Shu's soldiers run away like squirrels.

---

[1] Dai, La, Du, Ze, Meng, and En are monsters in Shu's warlike army.

黑白之战 // The War Between the Black and the White Tribes

阿璐是蛟龙，
站着神抖抖。
蛟龙闹海来，
黑鬼像泥鳅。

镇海大将军，
委给阿璐当。
派去白海边，
凭海设关防：

"东族不容侮，
东土不容犯。
术兵胆敢来，
牛刀斩鸡犬！"

遣兵侦察
The Spying of the Situation

Like a rampant dragon out of water,

Ahlu kicks and jumps in high spirits;

When he comes to the lake for a check,

Shu's soldiers waggle away like mud fish.

Appointed as General in Charge of the Lake,

Ahlu takes the post defined by Dong;

Along the banks of the frontier lake,

Passes are built for the goal of defense:

"Never should the White Tribe be insulted,

Nor should the land of Dong be invaded;

If Shu's soldiers dare come to invade,

They will fall victims to our choppers!

初战白海
The Lakeside Fighting

黑白之战 // The War Between the Black and the White Tribes

黑云聚白海,
沉沉像铜块。
术兵像蚂蚁,
涌向海子边。

黑气笼白海,
茫茫不见天。
术将像黑雕,
嚎着要叼羊。

长矛像乱蜂,
朝着阿璐戳;
长刀像闪电,
对着阿璐砍。

黑手像密林,
想把阿璐吞;
麻绳像花蛇,
要把阿璐捆。

阿璐施法术,

初战白海
The Lakeside Fighting

Dark clouds hanging over the white lake,
Cover the surface like copper lumps;
Shu's army, moving like swarms of ants,
Flows to the lake shore in huge columns.

The lake is engulfed by a dense fog,
And the sky overshadowed by clouds;
Shu's generals, moving like black hawks,
Vow to catch Ahlu, the bleating lamb.

Shu's invading soldiers, like buzzing wasps,
Thrust at Ahlu with long and sharp spears;
Shu's brutal men, quick as lightening,
Cut Ahlu with long and heavy knives.

Shu's soldiers, with hands like dense forests,
Vow to catch Ahlu, Dong's lovely son;
Shu's men, with ropes like long winding snakes,
Pledge to bind Ahlu, Dong's army leader.

Making use of his magic power,

黑白之战 // The War Between the Black and the White Tribes

海头弄旋风：
风势如狂龙，
风声如雷轰。

阿璐显神威，
海尾弄海波：
波狂像怒狮，
浪大像山峰。

飞身驾风浪，
浪立千丈高。
压向术兵群，
好像雪山倒。

术兵溃下去，
像河决了堤。
逃命嫌腿短，
爹妈喊不赢。

术将败下阵，
像城塌了门。
夺路乱相踩，
头也不敢回。

初战白海
The Lakeside Fighting

Ahlu creates a swirling wind over the lake:
Like a fierce dragon whirling around,
Or a thunder cracking overhead.

Demonstrating his invincible force,
Ahlu lifts waves over the huge lake:
Like ferocious lions prancing forward,
Or steep peaks dashing against the shore.

Riding on the storms like a captain,
Ahlu steers the bulky ship of waves;
Crashing on Shu's ant-like soldiers,
The waves engulf all like an avalanche.

Shu's soldiers retreat in disorder,
Like a rough river bursting the banks;
Dashing away for life on short legs,
They keep calling their parents for help.

Shu's generals, having lost the fight,
Fall back like a city without a gate;
Pushing forward for the escaping road,
They dare not turn around for a glance.

黑白之战 // The War Between the Black and the White Tribes

丹由压阵脚，
慌忙放妖箭。
箭头像冰雹，
纷纷落海面。

阿璐潜下海，
潜进九层殿。
阿璐掀大浪，
白浪高万丈。

术兵想过海，
海浪挡齐天；
术将想跨海，
有翅难飞天。

黑箭射海心，
好像鱼群游；
大浪作护盾，
难伤阿璐头。

术主干瞪眼，
自骂是蠢才。

初战白海
The Lakeside Fighting

To protect the rear part of his army,

Danyou shoots lethal arrows in haste;

But his arrowheads, dense as hailstones,

Fall onto the lake surface in vain.

Diving into the bottom of the lake,

Ahlu stays in the nine-storied hall;

Lifting mountains of towering waves,

Ahlu tries to block off his enemies.

Shu's soldiers want to cross the wide lake,

But they are walled off by the waves;

Shu's commanders want to cross the lake,

But regret that they are not birds with wings.

Arrows shot to the lake from Shu's men,

Float like swimming fish in the water;

But shielded by the huge and tall waves,

Ahlu remains safe at the lake bottom.

Unable to do anything about this,

Lord Shu curses himself for being an idiot;

黑白之战 // The War Between the Black and the White Tribes

丹由跺脚板，
像狗团团转。

低头定心想，
抬手抓抓腮；
想出一条计，
凑近术耳讲：

"捉鹰拿鸡诱，
伏虎拿兔引。
金钩钓好汉，
香饵是美人。"

风吹愁云散，
疙瘩顿解开。
术脸浮笑影，
术眼焕光彩。

初战白海
The Lakeside Fighting

Feeling rather worried and anxious,
Danyou keeps moving around in circles.

Lowering his head to think for a while,
And raising his hand to scratch his cheek,
Danyou comes up with a deadly trick.
Then he gets close to Lord Shu and whispers:

"To catch an eagle the chick is needed,
To trap a tiger the hare is used;
To fish for a great hero like Ahlu,
A pretty lady is the sure bait."

Like a wind blowing away the clouds,
Shu gets the knot untangled in his mind;
His face beams with a smile from ear to ear,
And his eyes shine with luster and light.

耿饶茨嫫
The Lure of Cimo

黑白之战 // The War Between the Black and the White Tribes

雪山长草乌,
也会开鲜花;
阴坡刺荨麻,
也会抽琼芽。

术主和纳嫫,
有女像枝花;
养育十八春,
长成像朵霞。

耿饶茨嫫呵,
美姿世上稀。
手似嫩竹笋,
腰似马蜂细。

纳嫫生九女,
茨嫫是心肝;
术主爱女儿,
明珠托在掌。

一觉睡得足,

耿饶茨嫫
The Lure of Cimo

Monkshoods may produce special blossoms,
Though poisonous they grow on snow hills;
Nettle smartweeds may give out tender shoots,
Though itching plants they are on shady slopes.

Lord Shu and his wife Gengrao Namo,
Are blessed with a beautiful daughter;
When the girl reaches her womanhood,
She looks prettier than the sunset glow.

Gengrao Cimo as she is thus named,
Whose complexion is rare in the world;
Her hands are like tender bamboo shoots,
And her waist like pliable willow twigs.

As the cutest among the nine sisters,
Cimo is the lamb of her mother;
As the most darling of her father,
Cimo is the apple in Lord Shu's eye.

She has a sound sleep every night,

黑白之战 // The War Between the Black and the White Tribes

三顿吃得饱；
山水任她游，
金银任她花。

术要钓鳌鱼，
拿她当饵子；
术要猎猛虎，
拿她当兔子。

银针缝金裙，
金剪裁银衣；
穿得像仙女，
扮得像妖精。

头发梳成辫，
发亮像玛瑙；
宝衣披在身，
飘动像彩霞。

听母夸奖话，
茨嫫喜心头；
听术悄悄话，
茨嫫心中愁。

耿饶茨嫫
The Lure of Cimo

And eats three good meals every day;

She goes to visit any place she loves,

And she spends money at her free will.

Now that Shu wishes to catch the turtle,

She is treated as the bait on his pole;

Now that Shu wants to hunt for the tiger,

She is taken as the prey for his game.

Her skirts are sewn with silver needles,

And her clothing cut with golden scissors;

When she puts on her fanciful dress,

She looks very much like a fairy.

When she has her hair done into plaits,

She looks like a large shining agate;

When she puts on her colorful dress,

She sails like a rosy cloud floating.

Hearing her mother's praise of Ahlu,

She feels delighted and full of joy;

Hearing of her father's sly whisper,

She is thrown into a worried state.

黑白之战 // The War Between the Black and the White Tribes

喜是会东子，
英名早传闻；
美人会好汉，
平生遂了心。

愁是会仇人，
不是会情人；
吉凶难预卜，
不知谁伏谁？

树木能生杈，
舌头难分枝；
只有一面脸，
难做两面人。

泥巴捏神尊，
随着匠手捏；
茨嫫像泥神，
任凭父母捏。

父旨不容悖，
母意难相违；

耿饶茨媄
The Lure of Cimo

She feels delighted because of meeting Ahlu,
A handsome prince with wide spread fame;
The fair and the brave make the right match,
The fine marriage she has long wished for.

She feels worried because of meeting a foe,
Rather than an innocent sweetheart;
None can foretell the actual outcome,
Nor can one predict the final winner.

Though the trunk of a tree may branch out,
The same is impossible for a tongue;
Since she has only one face to wear,
How can she be a double-faced woman?

Though the substance for statues is clay,
What they become is up to the craftsman;
Cimo's fate, like that of clay statues,
Is decided by her austere parents.

Father's arrangement must be followed,
Mother's intention must be observed;

黑白之战 // The War Between the Black and the White Tribes

不去不甘心,
要去又惊心。

半愁夹半喜,
半假藏半真,
驾起黑云彩,
急朝白海飞。

狐狸会骗人,
茨嫫要迷人;
刺藤会缠树,
茨嫫要缠人。

阿璐站海滨,
术兵逃无影。
风吹黑云降,
美人笑盈盈。

脸颊红润润,
好像堆胭脂;
牙齿白生生,
颗颗像糯米。

耿饶茨媶
The Lure of Cimo

Refusing the chance is against her will,
But taking the chance ventures a risk.

With mixed feelings of worried delight,
She finds herself in a half-minded state;
Riding on a large piece of black cloud,
She flies in haste toward the white lake.

Like a fox that deceives human beings,
Cimo intends to enchant Ahlu;
Like a vine twining about a tree,
Cimo decides to allure Ahlu.

Catching sight of Ahlu on the shore,
Shu's men run away without a trace;
Riding a wind-propelled dark cloud,
The fair beauty descends with a smile.

Her pretty cheeks look like pink roses,
Or like red rouge heaped up in piles;
Her teeth are white,
Like glutinous rice.

黑白之战 // The War Between the Black and the White Tribes

眼珠溜溜转,
流星滚天边;
衣摆随风荡,
一路喷喷香。

阿璐看呆了,
魂儿掉下井;
阿璐头晕了,
天地难分清。

呆了又吃惊,
晕了又清爽:
虎会学人话,
蛇会耍花圈。

莫非是术主,
派来美妖姬?
莫非是魔精,
有意来勾人?

阿璐低着头,
与她不通名,
像只小水獭,

耿饶茨蟆
The Lure of Cimo

Her bright watery eyes, when moving,
Are like meteors flashing across the sky;
The train of her skirt, floating in the wind,
Sends off perfume wherever she goes.

Being dumbfounded at Cimo's look,
Ahlu becomes a poor smitten cat;
Feeling crazy about Cimo's beauty,
He cannot tell heaven from earth.

Dumbfounded and crazy at one moment,
Clear, calm and shocked the next moment:
How come the tiger speaks like a man?
How come the snake plays with a garland?

Is it possible for Lord Shu,
To send a beauty for seduction?
Is it possible for a luring nymph,
To come for the trick of temptation?

Ahlu, lowering his head to his chest,
Holds back his wish of saying hello;
Looking like a frightened otter,

黑白之战 // The War Between the Black and the White Tribes

潜进碧水底。

茨嫫像饿鹰,
来回绕海飞。
轻呼柔声唤,
声声直揪心。

阿璐在海底,
偷看茨嫫影,
半天不眨眼,
半晌不呼吸:

绸衣衬缎袄,
如花衬绿叶;
绫袖配锦带,
如云烘明月。

彩丝拴发辫,
珍珠串头上,
金花插鬓边,
银蝶飞耳畔。

耳环坠腮根,

耿饶茨嫫
The Lure of Cimo

He dives deep into the lake bottom.

Cimo, looking like a hungry eagle,
Hovers the lake to hunt for her prey;
Calling for Ahlu in a soft voice,
She intends to pass her feeling to him.

Staying at the bottom of the lake,
Ahlu cannot help glancing at her;
Being too engaged to blink his eyes,
He even forgets to take a breath.

With her satin coat over a dress,
Cimo is a flower among green leaves;
With her silk belt and sleeves matched,
She is the moon veiled in a thin cloud.

Colored ribbons are used to bind her hair,
Pearl strings are used to adore her head,
Golden flowers are used as her hairpins,
And silvery butterflies as her pendants.

Earrings fall below her rosy cheeks,

黑白之战 // The War Between the Black and the White Tribes

项圈吊胸前，
玉镯套手腕，
戒指闪宝光。

珍宝照海水，
海水亮起来；
阿璐心儿呀，
跟着亮起来。

罗裙飘海水，
海波摇起来；
阿璐心儿呀，
跟着摇起来。

耿饶茨嫫
The Lure of Cimo

Necklaces reach out to her chest,

Jade bracelets circle her wrists,

And a ring flashes on her finger.

When the jewelry is reflected in the lake,

The lake water is aglow with light;

Ahlu's heart gets brighter and clearer,

With the brightening up of the lake.

When Cimo's skirt flutters on the lake,

The surface of the lake becomes chopping;

Ahlu's heart, likewise, starts pounding,

As he is enchanted with her charm.

阿璐上钩

The Hooking of Ahlu

黑白之战 // The War Between the Black and the White Tribes

勇猛山狮子,
会被猎狗哄;
能干好男子,
会被美人哄。

茨嫫唤千声,
海水起波纹;
茨嫫呼万声,
不闻阿璐音。

托腮想三回,
下海来梳洗,
披开墨玉发,
露出嫩脖颈。

伸出白手臂,
好像白玉梭,
穿飞在浪间,
纺丝织鲛罗。

一对白奶子,

阿璐上钩
The Hooking of Ahlu

A fierce lion, though brave and awesome,
Could be fooled and cheated by a hound;
A gifted man, though very competent,
Could be swindled or coaxed by a beauty.

Calling for Ahlu one thousand times,
Cimo sees only ripples on the lake;
Calling for Ahlu ten thousand times,
Cimo hears no reply from Ahlu.

Doing meditation with chin in her hands,
Cimo comes to take a wash of herself;
Pulling aside her pretty black hair,
Cimo exposes her soft tender neck.

When she stretches out her slim bright arms,
They look like loom shuttles of white jade;
When she does her washing in the ripples,
She seems to be weaving silk or satin.

Her white breasts

黑白之战 // The War Between the Black and the White Tribes

好像白蝴蝶,
停在浪花间,
轻轻颤翅膀。

边洗边歌唱,
歌声多委婉,
好像五色珠,
滚落在玉盘:

"天仙世无双,
来配英雄汉;
白鹤会青松,
来会好儿男。

"术兵早走尽,
好汉快出来;
银石陪金水,
来陪天女玩!"

阿璐变白鹰,
飞上白云端;
茨嫫变黑鹰,
追进白云间。

阿璐上钩
The Hooking of Ahlu

Look like two butterflies;

They rest among the waves,

And flutter with tender wings.

She sings while she is doing the wash,

And her voice is sweet and melodious,

Like the tinkling of colorful beads,

Which keep dropping on a jade plate.

"Like a goddess unmatched in this world,

She comes for a meeting with the hero;

Like a crane looking for a pine tree,

She comes for a meeting with her man.

"Shu's soldiers have been away for sure,

So please come out, my handsome young man;

As a fine match of silver and gold,

We are bound to be perfect partners!"

Changing himself into a white eagle,

Ahlu flies high up to the white clouds;

Changing herself into a black eagle,

Cimo follows him to the white clouds.

黑白之战 // The War Between the Black and the White Tribes

云丝悠悠绕，
云鹰双双飞，
情绵似云海，
缠绵在一起。

白鹰目光锐，
瞧见黑影子，
只怕术家网，
一闪钻海底。

青蛙到蛇口，
又被吓跑了；
黑鹰尖声叫，
术兵退远了。

蛇身蜕蛇鳞，
变成黄鳝跑；
茨嫫脱金衣，
下海来洗澡。

开襟露胸脯，
好似开白莲；

阿璐上钩
The Hooking of Ahlu

The clouds fly to embrace the eagles,

But the eagles glide and soar away;

Full of love like the lingering clouds,

The amorous couple toss and intertwine.

With eyes like bright penetrating balls,

The white eagle catches a black shadow;

Fearing the trap of Shu's unfolding net,

The bird dives into the lake bottom.

Like the frog escaping from a snake,

The white eagle is frightened away;

At the warning scream of the black eagle,

Shu's soldiers retreat farther away.

When all the scales of a snake come off,

It just looks like a soft eel in the pond;

When Cimo takes off her golden coat,

She returns to the lake for a bath.

When her breasts are revealed to the light,

They look like white lotuses in bloom;

黑白之战 // The War Between the Black and the White Tribes

哼起情歌调，
金嗓脆脆甜：

"一颗明星呀，
从天降下来。
落在白海边，
可惜没人睬。

"一朵鲜花呀，
云中飘下来。
谁有好福气，
鲜花落在怀。

"天上有仙女，
要配俊男子；
人间有好汉，
要伴美仙子。

"好汉阿璐呀，
仙子等你来。
快来配成双，
快来缔佳缘！"

阿璐上钩
The Hooking of Ahlu

Humming the pleasant tune of a love song,
Cimo's voice sounds so sweet and touching:

"A star is streaking across the sky,
Like a bright star with a long tail;
It draws no attention, a pity in fact,
Though landing on the shore of the lake.

"A fragrant flower in its prime of time,
Floats to the earth from the cloud above;
Who on earth is the most blessed one,
To fall in love with this girl of flower?

"A gorgeous fairy from heaven,
Should be matched with a handsome man;
A brave handsome young man on the earth,
Deserves the companion of a fairy.

"My most handsome young hero Ahlu,
Your fairy is here waiting for you;
Why don't you hurry to be her side,
And make a perfect match in this world?"

黑白之战 // The War Between the Black and the White Tribes

阿璐变白虎,
茨嫫变黑虎。
白虎前面行,
黑虎后面追。

翻了九架山,
不见术脚迹;
穿过七座林,
没有鬼气息。

白虎放了心,
陪着黑虎玩,
深林像蜂窝,
采情酿蜜浆。

清早玩到晚,
夜幕垂下天。
黑影惊虎心,
又到海底藏。

嗅着狐毛臭,
公鸡又惊飞。
到口不得吃,

阿璐上钩
The Hooking of Ahlu

Ahlu changes his form to a white tiger,
And Cimo changes hers to a black tiger;
The white tiger takes the lead in the front,
While the black tiger follows close behind.

Climbing over nine hills in a breath,
They discern no sign of Shu's army;
Getting through seven woods in a breath,
They notice no trace of Shu's soldiers.

Now feeling assured of his security,
The white tiger stays with his playmate;
Like a honeycomb for the bees to stay in,
The woods are ideal for the lovers.

They enjoy each other from morning till dusk,
When a curtain falls upon the trees;
Then shocked and startled at the dark shadow,
The white tiger goes back to the lake.

Smelling the nasty stink of a fox,
The rooster flies away in great fright;
Unable to have the prey in his mouth,

黑白之战 // The War Between the Black and the White Tribes

狐狸怎甘心?

茨嫫又洗澡,
头发像柳条。
赤脚戏碧波,
清喉又唱歌:

"哪有海上龙,
胆小像鲫鱼?
哪有金翅鹏,
怯懦似老鼠?

"是鱼是老鼠,
快去钻土窟;
是龙是大鹏,
快来会仙女!

"虎豹回山了,
蟒蛇归洞了。
有情来相会,
莫使我心焦。"

阿璐作变化,

阿璐上钩
The Hooking of Ahlu

How can the fox satisfy with the result?

Taking a second bath in the lake,

Cimo's hair flows like tender willows;

Touching waves with her delicate feet,

She clears her throat for another song:

"As a fierce dragon from the lake,

How could you act like a coward crucian?

As a soaring hawk with golden wings,

How could you be like a timid mouse?

"If you are a true crucian or mouse,

Go and stay in your hole as a coward;

If you are a real dragon or hawk,

Come and meet your fairy as a man.

"Tigers and leopards are in their dens,

And boas and snakes resort to their holes;

Come for a tryst if you love me true,

And never leave your girl in anxiety."

Making use of magic to change himself,

黑白之战 // The War Between the Black and the White Tribes

变头白牦牛；
茨媒作变化，
变头黑犏牛。

黑牛引白牛，
相随去嬉游；
高山游三夜，
不见术兵走。

山雾当罗帐，
山梁作眠床。
情长好做梦，
美梦多香甜。

白牛陪黑牛，
黑牛偎白牛，
深谷玩三天，
不见黑魔游。

谷深似酒瓮，
溪涧似米酒，
情意似酒浓，
狂饮醉悠悠。

阿璐上钩
The Hooking of Ahlu

Ahlu takes on the form of a white yak;
Making use of magic to change herself,
Cimo takes on the form of a black yak.

With the black one taking lead this time,
The yaks go on another joyful journey;
Traveling over on hills in three days,
They see not a Shu's soldier on patrol.

The fog makes up a fine bridal curtain,
And the ranges serve as natural beds;
Immersed in love they enjoy their sojourn,
And their dreams are beyond description.

The white yak consorts with the black yak,
And the black yak leans on the white yak;
Camping in the valley for three days,
They find not a Shu's man in roaming.

The fine valley looks like a wine jar,
And the stream in it is mellow wine;
With their amour more fragrant than wine,
They feel dizzy after a guzzle.

黑白之战 // The War Between the Black and the White Tribes

白天放宽心,
跟着茨媄行,
影子摞影子,
脚跟踩脚跟。

晚上壮了胆,
陪着茨媄玩,
耳朵擦耳朵,
巴掌抵巴掌。

走累并肩坐,
不觉太阳落;
坐累并排躺,
不知月亮落。

阿璐上钩
The Hooking of Ahlu

Relaxing himself in the daytime,

Ahlu keeps wandering with his love.

Their shadows overlap when they walk;

And their heels touch when they stroll.

Getting more audacious at twilight,

Ahlu employs more tricks for the game.

He touches Cimo's ears with his own

And presses his palms against Cimo's.

They sit side by side when tired of strolling,

Unaware of the setting sun at dusk;

They lie side by side when tired of sitting,

Unaware of the setting moon at night.

身陷魔窟
The Trapping of Ahlu

黑白之战 // The War Between the Black and the White Tribes

金鱼上了钩,
扯绳往上拉;
大路发了岔,
抬脚踩泥沼。

茨嫫对他说:
"我俩好侣伴,
天地美姻缘,
难找第二双。

"成对金鸳鸯,
要游好水塘;
成双银蝴蝶,
要绕好花园。

"有个好地方,
绿玉盖作天,
黄金铺作地,
银子铸山川。

"银树结宝果,
银鸡唱山歌,

身陷魔窟
The Trapping of Ahlu

When a goldfish is caught on the hook,
The fishing line should be yanked upward;
When confronted with divergent roads,
Ahlu decides to take the muddy one.

Then he hears Cimo whisper to him:
"Together we make a perfect couple,
And our marriage ranks highest in this world,
Second to none in my private view.

"As a fine pair of mandarin ducks,
We should choose to swim in a clear pond;
As a pair of loving butterflies,
We should hover in a nice garden.

"I know about a place in this world,
Where the sky is roofed with green jade,
The ground is covered with yellow gold,
And the hills and the rivers are forged from silver.

"Fruits of treasure are borne on trees,
Charming songs are chanted by roosters,

黑白之战 // The War Between the Black and the White Tribes

玉叶托金花,
金蝶绕花朵。

"石上长香草,
石下金水绕,
金狗汪汪叫,
成亲好安家。"

牛犊不知虎,
见虎会好笑;
阿璐呆一呆,
乐得眯眯笑:

"走过百条路,
蹚过百条河,
这般好地方,
平生没见过。

"世间无天堂,
乐土要寻找。
说的要是真,
愿去安新家。

"花不骗蜜蜂,

身陷魔窟
The Trapping of Ahlu

Flowers are cradled with jade petals,

And stamens are courted by butterflies.

"Above the rocks grow holy grasses,

Under the rocks flows golden water,

Barking nearby are some golden dogs,

What a nice place for our bridal home!"

Not knowing the traits of a tiger,

The calf finds it rather amusing;

With mind wandering for a moment,

Ahlu wears a grin over his face.

"Having traveled by a hundred roads,

And waded across a hundred rivers,

I have never seen a magical place,

More fanciful than this fairyland!

"There is no paradise in the world,

But a wonderland may merit a search;

If what you describe agrees with the facts,

It would be nice to build our home there.

"Flowers never fail to delight bees,

蜂不瞒鲜花。
情人不撒谎,
不信快去瞧。"

茨嫫来拉手,
阿璐心酥麻。
一步分两步,
好像蚯蚓爬。

爬上一座山,
茨嫫作法来:
绿玉铺高天,
金银铺山川。

树上银鸡唱,
花间金蝶旋,
金水绕香草,
金狗叫汪汪。

阿璐看实了,
阿璐信真了,
两步并一步,
像鹿跳着跑。

身陷魔窟
The Trapping of Ahlu

And bees never conceal their true love;
How can I tell a lie to my dearest lover,
And go for a look if you have a doubt!"

When touched by Cimo's tender hand,
Ahlu's desirous heart throbs faster;
Taking sluggish steps with his weak legs,
He moves forward like a crawling earth worm.

When they climb to the top of a hill,
Cimo begins to do more magic.
She first covers the sky with green jade,
And then the hills with gold and silver.

Roosters crow on the tall trees,
And butterflies flap among the flowers.
Water flows around the holy grasses,
While dogs bark in the neighborhood.

Having caught a good look at the scene,
Ahlu assures himself of the facts.
Merging two steps into a larger one,
Ahlu starts to jump up like a deer.

黑白之战 // The War Between the Black and the White Tribes

茨媒告诉他：
"前面更美好。
马鹿生银角，
山骡长金鬃。"

麻雀不知海，
见海要发懵；
阿璐像家雀，
好奇又惊愕：

"我家九代祖，
代代见识多；
我家七代宗，
万物都精通。

"这般稀奇事，
九代没见过；
这般妙光景，
七代没听过！"

再爬一座山，
茨媒又作法：
鹿角银闪闪，
山骡金鬃飘。

身陷魔窟
The Trapping of Ahlu

Yet Cimo manages to calm him down:
"The land ahead is more beautiful.
Silver horns grow out of red deer's heads,
And golden manes hang over mule's necks."

Having little knowledge about a lake,
A sparrow feels dumbstruck when seeing one;
Like the sparrow seeing little of the world,
Ahlu feels both startled and amazed.

"My forefather nine generations back,
Acquired profound knowledge of the world;
My forefather seven generations back,
Knew all the creatures on this planet.

"No animals so strange and rare like these,
Did they ever claim to have come across;
Or landscapes so fantastic like these,
Did they ever claim to have heard about."

Getting atop still another hill,
Cimo changes it to another wonder;
Ablaze are the silvery horns of red deer,
And the golden manes of mules are waving.

黑白之战 // The War Between the Black and the White Tribes

阿璐心花开,
停下要安家;
茨嫫手一摆,
把头摇三摇:

"前边更美妙,
石头会讲话,
树木会奔跑,
那里好安家。"

阿璐心儿跳,
好奇又好笑:
"酒里可掺水?
饭里可掺沙?"

"臭水不做汤,
真金不掺假,
情人心相照,
不信跑去瞧。"

茨嫫来拉他,
阿璐支开她;
三步并一步,

身陷魔窟
The Trapping of Ahlu

Feeling overjoyed with what he sees,

Ahlu stops to build their bridal home;

Seeing this Cimo waves her right hand,

And shakes her head like a rattling drum:

"There is a place still better ahead,

Where stones converse,

And trees run about,

That is the place for us to settle down."

With heart beating faster at the claim,

Ahlu finds it strange and amusing:

"Can we make more wine by adding water?

Or more cooked rice by adding sand?"

"Soup should not be cooked with smelly water,

And gold bars should not be cast impure;

Lovers should stay sincere first of all,

And go to check it if you have any doubt."

When Cimo gives him a helping hand,

Ahlu simply rejects her good will;

Putting three steps into a larger one,

黑白之战 // The War Between the Black and the White Tribes

双鸟飞天涯。

漩涡旋落花，
越旋越深了；
大风裹黄沙，
越裹越远了。

又翻九座山，
又跨七条谷。
石头在说话，
树木在走路。

阿璐看出神：
"这里把亲结？"
茨嫫暗暗乐：
"还要走一截。"

甑子蒸花卷，
开花在上面；
茨嫫嘴里甜，
心辣冒火烟。

躲过白的风，
避开白的云，

身陷魔窟
The Trapping of Ahlu

They roam afar like a pair of birds.

Like fallen petals in a whirlpool,
Ahlu falls deep into Cimo's trap;
Like sand blown away in a strong wind,
Ahlu is brought to a remote place.

Having climbed over nine huge mountains,
And waded across seven deep valleys;
They hear stones converse as humans do,
And see trees walk around as humans do.

Ahlu is enchanted by the strange scenes:
"Shall we get married and settle down here?"
Cimo replies with a restrained joy:
"We still have a short distance to walk."

When rolls are cooked in a steamer,
They get bulky on the top of the surface;
Despite the honey words from her mouth,
Cimo conceives a plot deep in her mind.

Shunning themselves from the white winds,
Shunning themselves from the white clouds,

黑白之战 // The War Between the Black and the White Tribes

走到交界处,
黑白见分明。

悄悄派黑风,
暗暗派黑云,
急急见术主,
匆匆报信音。

鳌鱼吞下钩,
有脚甩不脱;
阿璐中圈套,
有翅飞不脱。

米利术主来,
耿饶纳嫫来,
肯子丹由来,
一起细商量。

派出火烟鬼,
浓烟罩阿璐;
放出秽气鬼,
腥秽熏阿璐。

术兵上千来,

身陷魔窟
The Trapping of Ahlu

They come to the border between their tribes,
Where the Black and the White are in contrast.

Sending off the black Wind in secret,
Sending off the black Cloud in secret,
Cimo urges her messengers away
To Lord Shu for an instant report.

Like a fish stuck on a barbed hook,
Ahlu fails to get away on foot;
Like a bird caught in a trapping net,
Ahlu fails to fly away with wings.

Lord Mili Shu arrives for the gathering,
Gengrao Namo arrives for the gathering,
Kendzi Danyou comes for gathering,
Together they are making a plan.

Sending out the Smoke Ghost for a task,
They wish to choke Ahlu with thick smog;
Sending out the Odor Ghost for a task,
They wish to numb Ahlu with foul air.

Thousands of Shu's soldiers come up

黑白之战 // The War Between the Black and the White Tribes

八方困阿璐；
术将上百来，
四面围阿璐。

脚上钉铁镣，
手上戴铁铐；
茨嫫发苦笑，
阿璐怒火烧。

羊子进虎穴，
莫想再求饶；
人到对头家，
有仇不相饶。

要悔不及悔，
要拼不得拼，
想起爹和妈，
热泪像抛沙。

身陷魔窟
The Trapping of Ahlu

To encircle Ahlu from all sides;
Hundreds of Shu's generals come up
To surround Ahlu from all directions.

Ahlu's feet are locked in shackles,
And his hands locked in iron cuffs.
Catching a wry smile on Cimo's face,
He finds himself burning in anger.

Once a lamb enters the tiger's den,
He finds it useless to beg for mercy;
When a man meets with his enemy,
He has no way to ask for pardon.

With no means to undo his actions,
Nor a way to fight against his foes,
Ahlu keeps thinking of his parents,
And sheds regretful tears like grains of sand.

术兵犯境
The Invasion of Shu's Soldiers

黑白之战 // The War Between the Black and the White Tribes

蜂窝失蜂王,
蜂群会乱飞;
白海失守将,
东兵不成军。

牧场无牧人,
羊群会乱跑;
东兵失统帅,
打仗乱如麻。

海里无蛟龙,
浪平好行船;
丹由驱术兵,
轻易渡海来。

山中无老虎,
有柴随意砍;
术兵闯东境,
凶狠像虎狼。

白天东在家,

术兵犯境
The Invasion of Shu's Soldiers

When the honeycomb loses its queen bee,
The swarm do their flight in a blind way;
When the White Tribe loses its general,
Dong's soldiers are in great disorder.

When the sheep stays not on the pasture,
They may scatter in all directions;
When Dong's army loses its high leader,
They can stage but a messy fighting.

With no dragon to guard the white lake,
It becomes smooth and calm for sailing;
Taking his troops in large sailing boats,
Danyou drives his men across the lake.

With no tiger to guard the mountains,
The woods are left at cutter's mercy;
Killing and looting along their route,
Shu's men become fierce wolves and tigers.

During his stay at home in the daytime,

黑白之战 // The War Between the Black and the White Tribes

眼皮跳三跳；
晚上东上床，
噩梦绕三绕：

梦见火烧房，
梦见水冲田，
梦见蛇吞蛙，
梦见狼叼羊。

黑云阵阵滚，
涌向白云天；
黑风声声啸，
扑进白林间。

探子来报警，
守将来告急：
"阿璐失踪了，
术兵杀来了！"

东主传令符，
吹起海螺号，
擂响牛皮鼓，
忙把兵马调。

术兵犯境
The Invasion of Shu's Soldiers

Dong's eyelids twitch thrice as an ill sign;

During his sleeping hours deep at night,

He is haunted by some horrible dreams:

Houses on flaring fires are dreamed of,

Farmlands in sweeping floods are dreamed of,

Serpents gobbling down frogs are dreamed of,

And lambs taken by wolves are dreamed of.

Black clouds rolling and rumbling forward,

Surge high up toward the white heaven;

Black winds roaring and whistling forward,

Blow against the twigs of the white woods.

The scout dashes in for a quick report,

And the guard comes for an alarm in haste:

"Ahlu our commander is missing,

And the enemy troops are coming!"

Seeing the symbol of war from Lord Dong,

Dong's soldiers blow bugles of conch shells;

Beating drums of cowhide as signals,

They make their war deployment in haste.

黑白之战 // The War Between the Black and the White Tribes

火来才舀水，
有水舀晚了；
水来才筑堤，
有堤难保了。

垭口战三场，
乱麻绞成团。
黑剑碰白剑，
满山爆火光。

坡头战三场，
草坡秃脊梁。
黑箭撞白箭，
遍坡雷声喧。

路上战三天，
尘土飞满天。
刀口成锯齿，
盔甲变破筛。

寨前战三天，
浓烟像雾海。

术兵犯境
The Invasion of Shu's Soldiers

To scoop water to put out a wild fire,

It'll be too late when the event happens;

To build a dike to stop a rushing flood,

It'll be too late when the hazard occurs.

With three rounds of fighting at the pass,

The soldiers from both sides are intermingled;

When their swords bump against each other,

Sparkle flashes out over the steep hillside.

With three rounds of fighting on the slope,

The verdant ranges have been striped bare;

When the arrows thump against each other,

Thundering clangs are heard over the slope.

With three days of fighting on the route,

Whirling dust and dirt permeate the air;

The swords becomes jagged due to slashes,

And the armor full of holes due to thrusts.

With three days of fighting near the camps,

The field is shrouded in a sea of dark clouds;

黑白之战 // The War Between the Black and the White Tribes

汗水流满井,
血水淌成江。

垭口守不住,
山坡守不住,
路上斗不赢,
寨前斗不赢。

有将阵亡了,
有兵战死了,
不得不退了,
不得不撤了。

米利东主呀,
父亲是天族。
他要躲战祸,
暂且去天宫。

色爪苟嫫呀,
是东小女儿;
跑到白山上,
躲进深谷里。

术兵犯境
The Invasion of Shu's Soldiers

Sweat falling off the soldiers forms ponds,
And blood from the wounds creates streams.

The fierce fighting at the pass is in vain,
The fierce fighting on the slope is in vain,
The fierce fighting on the route is in vain,
And that near the camp is also in vain.

Most of the generals have been killed,
Most of the soldiers have been killed,
So the rest soldiers have to run for lives,
And carry out Dong's order to retreat.

Alas, Lord Mili Dong,
Whose father resides in heaven;
To avoid the fate of being captured,
He takes refuge in the Palace of Heaven.

Oh, Princess Sezhua Goumo,
The youngest daughter of Lord Mili Dong;
Climbing up to a hill on the white land,
She takes refuge in a bushy cavern.

黑白之战 // The War Between the Black and the White Tribes

依古根库呀,
是东小儿子;
跑到白峰头,
躲进岩缝里。

五谷搬上山,
六畜吆上山;
珍珠埋岩间,
宝石埋岩间。

金嫫是龙族,
儿舅在海宫。
战火她不怕,
不愿去龙宫:

"坏事有百样,
我没做一件。
做事不亏心,
半夜心不惊。

"术有千斤石,
不能压死我!
术有千把刀,

术兵犯境
The Invasion of Shu's Soldiers

Oh, Prince Yigu Genku,

The youngest son of Lord Mili Dong;

Climbing up to a peak on the white land,

He hides himself in a rock crevice.

Bags of grain are taken up to the hills,

And livestock is driven up to the hills;

Pearls are buried in some rock crevices,

And other treasures are also concealed.

Coming from the dragon species,

Jinmo used to live in the lake bottom;

Not afraid of being held as captive,

She refuses to take refuge in the lake.

"Though evils in this world are countless,

None of them can be attributed to me;

Always heeding my good conscience,

I have a soft pillow for my sleep.

"Having a rock of a thousand pounds,

Lord Shu finds no cause to place it on me!

Even if he has a thousand swords,

黑白之战 // The War Between the Black and the White Tribes

怎敢杀死我！"

黑鹰飞来了，
黑豹跑来了，
黑虎扑来了，
黑牛撞来了。

丹由射黑箭，
左普挥大刀，
季登举利斧，
斥补舞尖矛。①

嚎着要捉东，
东走不留针；
想擒东儿女，
汗毛无一根。

黑绳捆金嫫，
术主审金嫫；
"东主去哪里？
珠宝藏哪里？"

---

① 季登：术将罗霸季登；斥补：术将哈拉斥补。

术兵犯境
The Invasion of Shu's Soldiers

Does he dare to kill me on a pretext?"

Here come the black eagles flying fast,
Here come the black leopards dashing fast,
Here come the black tigers swooping fast,
And the black oxen hurtling fast, too.

Danyou is shooting arrows from the back,
Zuopu is waving his large broadsword,
Jideng is raising up his sharp axe,
And Chibu is wielding his keen spear.①

Shu's men howl out their desire to seize Dong,
But they find nothing at all left behind;
Shu's men vow to capture Dong's daughter,
But they find not single trace left behind.

When Jinmo is tied with a strong rope,
She is questioned by Lord Shu himself:
"Where does Lord Dong hide himself?
And where does he hide his treasures?"

---

① Jideng is the short form for Luoba Jideng, one of Shu's generals; Chibu is the short form for Hala Chibu, also one of Shu's generals.

黑白之战 // The War Between the Black and the White Tribes

指着白山问,
一问九摇头;
指着白海问,
九问不点头。

黑鞭像雨雪,
纷纷落满头;
翠竹不折腰,
金嫫不低头!

术兵乱砍杀:
老的站着杀,
小的睡着杀,
壮的追着杀。

烧房捉牛羊,
成群往回赶;
砸柜搜金银,
成箩往回抬。

白房白院里,
黑气冲上来;

術兵犯境
The Invasion of Shu's Soldiers

To Shu's questions about the white mountains,

Jinmo responds with a shake of her head;

To Shu's questions about the white lake,

She never gives a nod as her reply.

Like the sudden shower of a heavy hail,

Shu's whippings drop upon Jinmo's head;

Like a bamboo withstanding the wind,

Jinmo refuses to give any information!

A slaughter is committed by Shu's men:

The elderly are killed while standing,

The young are killed while sleeping,

And the middle-aged are killed while fleeing.

They burn down shelters for cattle and sheep,

And drive herds of livestock to their homes;

They smash open cupboards for treasures,

And take home full baskets of trophies.

From the courtyards on the white land,

Dark smoke rises high up to heaven;

黑白之战 // The War Between the Black and the White Tribes

白田白地上，

黑幕盖下来。

术兵犯境
The Invasion of Shu's Soldiers

Over the crop fields on the white land,

An immense screen is seen coming down.

宁死不屈
The Unyielding of Ahlu

黑白之战 // The War Between the Black and the White Tribes

术兵押阿璐,
蹚过九条河,
穿过九个坝,
爬过九座坡。

尼青肯乌寨,
是术大本营。
阿璐押过来,
关在铁屋里。

墙上安铜刺,
墙根插铁针。
纳补乌吕① 呵,
守住铁房门。

黑羊守城上,
黑鱼守城下,
獠牙瘦黑狗,
守在城半腰。

---

① 纳补乌吕:男看守名。

宁死不屈
The Unyielding of Ahlu

Ahlu, held as a prisoner of war,

Is forced to wade across nine rivers,

Traverse nine flat lands without pause,

And climb up nine slopes without a rest.

Being taken to Niqing Kenwu,

The general camp for Shu's army,

He is thrown into an iron room,

And kept as a prisoner of war.

The walls are embedded with copper thorns,

And the base is armed with iron needles;

Nabu Wulü[①], Shu's chief prison guard,

Is assigned to guard the door.

The black Goat guards at the top of the tower,

The black Fish guards at the foot of the tower,

And the black Dog with his snarling teeth,

Patrols the middle section of the tower.

---

① Nabu Wulü is a male prison guard in Shu's army.

黑白之战 // The War Between the Black and the White Tribes

术要报儿仇，
扯弓嗡嗡响；
术要杀阿璐，
磨刀霍霍响。

东天有日月，
术想夺过来；
东地有光明，
术想抢过来。

术要东天黑，
术要东地暗；
术要术天明，
术要术地亮。

摘取日和月，
秘诀要通晓。
术主没料到，
术主不知晓。

松开射人弓，
收起砍头刀。
嫁女嫁对头，

宁死不屈
The Unyielding of Ahlu

Anxious to take revenge for his son,

Shu pulls the bow back with a jerk;

To put his foe to death with a sharp knife,

He grinds his broadsword with a loud noise.

As for the sun and the moon in Dong's sky,

Shu wishes to take them home by force;

As for the luminous lights on Dong's land,

He wishes to take them home by force.

He wishes his enemy a dark sky,

And a murky land to go with it;

He wishes his kinsmen a clear sky,

And a radiant land to go with it.

But to take hold of the sun and the moon,

One has to know the password at first;

Shu is then forced to change his trick,

For he is ignorant of those secrets.

So he puts his bow back into its case,

And his broadsword into its scabbard;

Making use of his daughter's marriage,

黑白之战 // The War Between the Black and the White Tribes

枕边套秘法。

茨嫫钦好汉,
真情有三分;
好汉是仇敌,
真情难相倾。

父旨嫁阿璐,
真喜有七分;
吉凶难卜知,
惊怕有三分。

竹篾编篮子,
凭着竹匠编;
茨嫫像篾条,
只好凭父编。

家狗怕主人,
不敢不听话;
囡像妈的狗,
只好听妈话。

真情夹虚情,

宁死不屈
The Unyielding of Ahlu

He regards it as a workable trick.

Admiring Ahlu as a great hero,
Cimo has true affection for him;
But since he is from the hostile tribe,
Her love for him is half restrained.

Though married through her dad's arrangement,
Cimo feels delighted on the whole;
But unsure of her marital outcome,
She finds it worrisome to some degree.

When the craftsman weaves a basket,
He has many ways for his own choice;
Like the splints for bamboo weaving,
Cimo leaves her decisions to her dad.

When a dog is fed by its owner,
He is supposed to follow orders;
Like a puppy raised up by her mom,
Cimo has to be an obedient child.

Showing a pretentious love for her man,

黑白之战 // The War Between the Black and the White Tribes

茨嫫来温存。
开镣当新婿,
阿璐难解谜:

昨日阶下囚,
何因成上宾?
莫非茨嫫她,
果是抱真心?

不辨假与真,
和美做夫妻。
水滴融乳汁,
相融在梦里。

茨嫫好话儿,
像根糖绳子。
要捆阿璐心,
要把秘诀引:

"你是我的心,
你是我的肝;
我有心肝话,
你来听我讲。

宁死不屈
The Unyielding of Ahlu

Cimo looks much meeker than a lamb.

When taken as the groom without fetters,

Ahlu feels puzzled at his change of fate:

Being held a prisoner till last night,

Why is he treated as a guest this morning?

Could it be for the sake of Cimo,

Who might have truly fallen in love?

With no need to tell the true from false,

They enjoy their love to the extreme;

Living in harmony as man and wife,

They are lovers enchanted with dreams.

The soothing words uttered by Cimo,

Form a string coated with brown sugar;

They are whispered to Ahlu as a lure,

For his unconscious release of the password:

"Oh Ahlu, my talented darling,

You are the tender part of my heart;

For you I have a good suggestion,

And I wonder if I could have your ear.

黑白之战 // The War Between the Black and the White Tribes

"父亲好心肠,
金山要给你;
母亲好脾气,
银海要送你。

"说出口诀来,
讲出秘语来,
抱住金银山,
万年享不完!"

跌过一回井,
再来就小心;
落过一次网,
再来就警惕。

日月连着心,
故乡连着肝;
心肝不能丢,
秘诀不能讲:

"岩头金马鹿,
看见灵芝草;

宁死不屈
The Unyielding of Ahlu

"As a man endowed with a kind heart,
Dad plans to reward you with his gold;
As a lady with generous traits,
Mum wishes to give you all her silver.

"Tell me the secret of the bright lights,
Along with that of the stars as well;
Then you'll be rewarded with treasure,
For an affluent life in the coming years!"

Having once been trapped in a well,
Ahlu now becomes more vigilant;
Having once been captured in a net,
He grows more alert to such occasions.

Missing the sun and the moon so much,
Ahlu holds his native land so dear;
How can he tell the password to his foes,
For the treasure as he is promised of?

"Like a red deer grazing on the rock,
I got trapped by the charm of Cimo;

黑白之战 // The War Between the Black and the White Tribes

跑去嚼灵芝，
哪知是毒草。

"一次被蛇咬，
再次见蛇怕。
秘诀我不说，
你莫耍花招。"

茨嫫劝阿璐，
九次劝不回；
茨嫫哄阿璐，
九法哄不成。

再劝口干了，
再哄没话了。
茨嫫刚走开，
丹由又上前：

"你是祭神羊，
拴在木桩上；
你是过年鸡，
罩在竹篮里。

宁死不屈
The Unyielding of Ahlu

She looked prettier than a snow lotus,
Though a poisonous flower in disguise.

"Once bitten by a venomous snake,
I have become watchful ever since;
Resolved not to let out the password,
I pledge never to be taken in."

Refusing to be talked into coming around,
Ahlu seems deaf to Cimo's preaching;
Refusing to be coaxed and swindled,
Ahlu seems immune to Cimo's tricks.

With no more means for her persuasion,
Nor proper diction for her desired coaxing,
Cimo simply gives up and walks away,
Before Danyou comes to take her place.

"Like the goat fastened to a stake,
You are doomed to be sacrificed;
Like the rooster caged in a basket,
You will be killed on New Year's Eve.

黑白之战 // The War Between the Black and the White Tribes

"说出秘诀来,
留命在人间;
若想硬碰硬,
当作死鼠埋!"

阿璐想太阳,
阿璐念月亮。
想东青青草,
念东肥牛羊:

"东地有甘泉,
千股万股淌;
东地有日月,
千年万年亮。

"宁可饮毒水,
宁可一人死,
不让甘泉枯,
不让光明毁!"

阿璐泪流尽,
心似石头坚;
火烧石头炸,

宁死不屈
The Unyielding of Ahlu

"Speak out the secrets,

You might be granted a longer life;

But if you choose to be a tough guy,

You will be buried alive like a rat!"

Missing his home in a fond way,

Ahlu longs to see the the sun and the moon,

The pasture so verdant back in his home,

And the herds of cattle and sheep as well.

"The fountains and springs taste so sweetish,

The streams and creeks flow across the land;

The sun and the moon give off bright light,

To brighten Dong's land for eternity.

"I'd take the risk of drinking hemlock,

Or even take poison to end my life,

Rather than to lose the sweet fountains,

Or ruin the radiance of our lamps."

Having shed all his tears for his home,

Ahlu hardens his heart into a rock;

Even if a rock could explode in flames,

黑白之战 // The War Between the Black and the White Tribes

心儿炸不开。

阿璐绝饮食,
身似耍木坚;
木头会晒裂,
身子晒不干。

丹由来威吓,
七十七次逼;
阿璐心儿硬,
七十七次顶:

"快来杀我吧,
东族不怕死!
术要摘日月,
除非狗变鸡!"

宁死不屈
The Unyielding of Ahlu

But never will his rock-hardened heart.

To protest against Shu's imprisonment,
Ahlu, like a wood block, rejects any food;
Even if a wood block could crack in the sun,
But never would Ahlu be warmed up.

Danyou has conducted his menacing threats
For seventy seven times at least;
And Ahlu has put up his resistance
For seventy seven times also.

"Come and kill me to fulfill your dream,
And to me death is nothing to be dreadful!
You can never take away our bright lamps,
Unless you can turn a dog into a chick!"

茨嫫忏悔
The Remorse of Cimo

黑白之战 // The War Between the Black and the White Tribes

术主假嫁女,

娃娃真的生:

罗池是哥哥,

罗沙是弟弟。①

三年又三月,

阿璐关屋里;

罗沙和罗池,

屋边来游戏。

罗池问看守:

"屋里关哪个?"

乌吕笑呵呵:

"是你老祖宗。"

罗沙问母亲:

"黑屋关的谁?"

茨嫫笑且悲:

"是你真父亲。"

---

① 罗池:全名哈补罗池;罗沙:全名哈补罗沙。

The Remorse of Cimo

Though married through her dad's arrangement,
Cimo gives birth to kids of her own will.
The elder son is given the name Luochi,
While the younger one is called Luosha. ①

For a period of three years and three months,
Ahlu has been locked in a dark room;
Now when the two kids are old enough,
They come to play games close to his room.

Luochi raises a question to the guard:
"Who on earth is kept in the dark room?"
Wulv the guard replies with a grin:
"One of your old uncles, I should say."

Luosha asks his mom the same question:
"Who on earth is locked in the dark room?"
Cimo answers him with a wry smile:
"He is your real father, I should say."

---

① Luochi is the short form for Habu Luochi; Luosha is the short form for Habu Luosha.

听儿问话声,
阿璐细思忖。
给儿唱个歌,
让儿去报信:

"夜空星星呀,
是天好儿孙;
我的孩子呀,
是东后代孙。

"铮铮硬骨头,
东族给了你;
圣洁血与肉,
东族塑成你。

"东地有太阳,
东地有月亮,
遍野长青草,
满山跑牛羊。

"参天百年树,
落叶要归根;
东族好子孙,

茨嫫忏悔
The Remorse of Cimo

Hearing his elder son's naive question,
Ahlu conceives a plan in his mind:
His story can be sung to his child,
Who may go to Dong to give a report:

"The stars that twinkle in the dark sky
Are members of the heavenly family;
And my dear son, in terms of kinship,
Is a direct descendant of Lord Dong.

"The strong bones that support your body
Are endowed to you by your great tribe;
And the blood and flesh that make you up
Are gifts from your holy ancestors.

"In our homeland we have the bright sun,
And the moon that shines on a dark night;
Green pastures extend into the distance,
Over which herds of cattle and sheep graze.

"The fallen leaves of an aged tall tree
Are expected to gather around its root;
As a descendant of the great Lord Dong,

黑白之战 // The War Between the Black and the White Tribes

快回东家里！"

乌吕听见了，
急忙撵孩子；
乌吕害怕了，
慌忙告主子：

"家畜和野兽，
吃草不同窝；
主人和冤家，
喝茶不同桌。

"阿璐像核桃，
咬他反断牙。
秘诀死不说，
茨嫫白嫁他。

"白天怕他唱，
夜晚怕他逃。
不如杀了他，
免得把心焦。"

术主点点头，

茨姆忏悔
The Remorse of Cimo

You should unite with His Excellency!"

Hearing Ahlu's agitating song,
Wulv drives off the child in haste;
Being afraid of Ahu's stirring story,
He runs to his master to give a report:

"Livestock and beasts should never be kept
In the same barn for raising or breeding;
Nor should our master invite his foe
To drink tea at the one and same table.

"One may hurt his teeth to crack a nut,
And for us, Ahlu is a tougher nut;
Keeping his secrets with a strong will,
He pays nothing for his fine marriage.

"We fear him singing in the daytime,
And we fear him escaping at deep night.
So we might as well get rid of him
To keep ourselves away from worry."

Nodding his head in a thoughtful way,

黑白之战 // The War Between the Black and the White Tribes

喊来刀斧手。
阿璐被捆绑,
押去黑海边。

左普来砍头,
毒兵来提头,
黑蚁来喝血,
黑蝶来吮油。

凶信如冰风,
刮得茨嫫抖。
嫁时像儿戏,
死别情难舍:

"把我嫁阿璐,
为何杀阿璐?
要儿变遗孤?
要我当寡妇?

"骗他是茨嫫,
骗我是父母;
相骗到头来,
噩梦做一场!"

茨嫫忏悔
The Remorse of Cimo

Lord Shu calls right then for his executioner.

Having his foe tied up with a rope,

He orders him to be taken to the lake.

Zuopu carries out the death penalty,

Dubing hurries to pick up the head,

Swarms of black ants come to suck the warm blood,

And flocks of black butterflies gather for the fat.

Hearing the awful news of her man,

Cimo trembles beyond her control;

She used to take her marriage as a game,

But now she is unable to face his death:

"You arranged for me to marry Ahlu,

But why do you kill him in cruelty?

Do you wish to make my sons orphans?

And your daughter a helpless widow?

"I am to blame for coaxing Ahlu,

But you are cheaters to your daughter;

When the deception is carried out,

It results in a torturing nightmare!"

黑白之战 // The War Between the Black and the White Tribes

茨嫫到海滨,
含泪瞟亲人。
面对刽子手,
忏悔放悲声:

"我爱阿璐脸,
美似日月圆;
我慕阿璐能,
巧工能开天。

"曾是真对头,
曾是假夫妻;
对头会变亲,
假也会变真。

"生儿同养育,
哪能不生情?
魔心也是肉,
哪能不动心?

"骗他我有计,
救他我无能。

茨媄忏悔
The Remorse of Cimo

Coming to the shore of Mili Daji,

Cimo casts a glance at her husband;

Turning around to face the butcher,

She makes her confession in a sad voice:

"What I envy most is Ahlu's face,

A plate rounder than the sun or the moon;

What I admire is Ahlu's talent,

A fabulous skill to amend the sky.

"We were enemies at the outset,

Or rather a false couple in reality;

But enemies may become intimate,

And a false couple may become real.

"We share the duty of raising sons,

How can we hold back our true feelings?

Even a devil may have a heart,

How can a couple remain aloof?

"To cheat Ahlu I used all my tricks,

But to rescue him I have no means;

黑白之战 // The War Between the Black and the White Tribes

恨只恨父亲,
恨只恨自己。

"你们要杀他,
我只求个愿:
莫使三滴血,
染污他的脸。

"生难一同老,
死要一路行。
害他我有份,
他死我来陪!"

雷声轰一轰,
电光闪一闪,
茨嫫夺剑柄,
殉情在一旁。

黑海刮黑风,
黑海翻黑波,
黑风卷黑波,
一片黑蒙蒙!

茨姆忏悔
The Remorse of Cimo

I have no one to resent but my dad,
And I could blame no one but myself.

"Before you do the execution,
I have got a small wish to make:
I do hope that Ahlu's pretty face
Would never be smeared by his blood.

"Unable to grow old as his partner,
I will go with him on the road to death;
Since he is trapped because of my tricks,
I must follow him on the road to death."

A thunderclap sounds in the distance,
And lightning flashes in the darkness;
Snatching the sword all of a sudden,
Cimo cuts her throat for the sake of love.

Dark winds are howling over the lake,
Dark waves are marching across the lake;
When the two forces meet each other,
They create a world that is as dark as pitch.

东主返世
The Return of Lord Dong

黑白之战 // The War Between the Black and the White Tribes

白光照白云，
东主天上回。
脚踩焦土地，
手摸破烂堆。

渠里流着血，
山里抛着尸。
小孩失父母，
老人丢儿孙。

荒墟不生草，
干坡不淌泉。
太阳少光彩，
月亮多凄凉。

东主来回走，
心痛像刀绞；
母虎失乳子，
眼泪像雨浇。

东主上下瞧，

东主返世
The Return of Lord Dong

Riding a cloud aglow in the sunshine,
Lord Dong returns home from heaven;
Placing his feet on the scorched land,
He caresses the debris on his land in sorrow.

Blood is heard gurgling in the ditches,
And bodies are discarded in the wilderness;
Kids were orphaned when their parents died,
And the old are lonely when the young are killed.

No green grass grows on the wasteland,
Nor any spring flows on the dry slopes;
The sun loses all its brilliant lights,
And the moon becomes chilly and cold.

Wandering back and forth restlessly,
Lord Dong feels an acute pain in his heart;
Like a tiger whose cub was killed ,
He fails to hold back his bitter tears.

Looking around at his ravaged land,

黑白之战 // The War Between the Black and the White Tribes

心窝像锤打；
羊圈遭灾殃，
豺狼不可饶！

高高一座山,
树木全烧光。
老人下山来,
歌声多哀婉：

"老羊失小羊,
不想吃草了;
羊毛被烧光,
羊要冻死了。"

上前扶老者,
热手烫冰肠：
"刀仇要刀报,
血债要血偿！"

长长一条河,
满河扬怒波。
青年聚河滩,
歌声多激昂：

东主返世
The Return of Lord Dong

Lord Dong feels a severe pain in his heart;
For their crime of assaulting the sheep,
The jackals can never be forgiven.

This verdant hill once covered with woods
Has become bald when the trees were burnt.
Coming down the hill as a survivor,
An old shepherd sings a sad song:

"Watching the slaughter of their babies,
The ewes refuse to take in any grass;
With their thick fur burnt to ashes,
They would freeze to death in cold winter."

Attacking the enemy to help the survivor,
Lord Dong comforts him with a solemn oath:
"Killing should be repaid with killing,
And blood avenged with blood only!"

This river which once hummed a song
Has become angry with surging waves;
And the youth gathered by the bay
Are singing in a majestic chorus:

黑白之战 // The War Between the Black and the White Tribes

"黑魔不久长,
光明要回来,
黑夜虽漫长,
星星在发光。

"不敢斩魔鬼,
不算英雄汉;
杀退术家兵,
家园要重建。

"东族弟兄呀,
快来拉弓弦;
东族姐妹呀,
快来搬石块。

"飞到术天去,
救回亲人来;
冲进术地去,
夺回牛羊来!"

歌声像火塘,
东主解了冻;

东主返世
The Return of Lord Dong

"Dark evil can never exist for long,

For the lights would surely be restored;

Though the nights may prevail for some time,

The stars will without doubt take their place.

"People who dare not kill the evil,

Should never be counted as heroes;

United we will drive away the enemy,

With the aim of rebuilding our homes.

"You angry brothers of the White Tribe,

Come and pull back the bows of archers;

You wrathful sisters of the White Tribe,

Come and pile rocks for the coming fight.

"Shoot the arrows at Shu's soldiers,

To bring back our relatives and kinsmen;

Plunge into the land of the Black Tribe,

To take back our flocks of sheep and cattle!"

Like a huge fire that flames within a stove,

Their singing restores hope to Lord Dong's heart;

黑白之战 // The War Between the Black and the White Tribes

歌声像蜜水，
东主解了渴。

山头竖火把，
火光召人归；
山脚吹牛角，
角声唤亲回。

金嫫逃回来，
苟嫫出山来，
根库下岩来，
兵将聚拢来。

死灰有了火，
枯井有了水，
焦土有了芽，
哑嗓有了声！

东主返世
The Return of Lord Dong

Like a drink made of honey and water,

Their singing quenches Lord Dong's lasting thirst.

Torches are lit on the peak of the hill,

As signals to assemble the fighters;

Horns are blown at the foot of the hill,

As urgent calls to bring back the tribesmen.

Jinmo comes back to answer the call,

Goumo comes back to answer the call,

Genku comes back to answer the call,

And the troops also come back at the call.

Sparks keep cracking in the embers,

Water keeps gushing in the dry well,

And bushes keep sprouting out of the scorched earth,

Like miraculous sounds from the mute!

祖孙相逢
The Reunion of Lord Dong's Family

黑白之战 // The War Between the Black and the White Tribes

战场升炊烟,
东地庆团圆。
阿璐独不归,
如刺卡心间。

东主盼儿子,
一天盼不来,
一月盼不来,
一年盼不来。

四面找过了,
上下找过了,
中间找过了,
阿璐不见了。

一天遇千人,
怎不遇阿璐?
一夜梦百人,
怎不梦阿璐?

找到若倮山,

祖孙相逢
The Reunion of Lord Dong's Family

Fire smoke is seen arising from the battle field,

And Dong's people are cheering for their reunion;

Yet the only pity is Ahlu's absence,

Which is like a thorn stuck in Dong's throat.

Lord Dong has been expecting to see his son,

And he holds it fast to his fond dream;

Waiting is what he does all the while,

Till months and seasons have passed by.

All directions have been looked carefully,

All caverns have been surveyed thoroughly,

All jungles have been searched in detail,

But still Ahlu is nowhere to be found.

Lord Dong comes across thousands of his men,

But why is his son not among them?

Hundreds of figures appear in his dream,

But why is his son not among them?

Going to Mount Ruoluo for an answer,

黑白之战 // The War Between the Black and the White Tribes

叩问山和谷。
神山不说话,
神谷默无语。

找到达吉海,
叩问宝达树。
海不应一声,
树不答一句。

泪下如冰雹,
山虎震天啸:
"我儿阿璐呀,
莫非被术杀?"

喊声化海涛,
喊声荡云霄,
罗池听见了,
罗沙听见了。

躲过黑云手,
瞒过黑风眼,
哈补两兄弟,
跑到东地来。

祖孙相逢
The Reunion of Lord Dong's Family

Lord Dong asks and begs the mountain for help;

But the sacred mountain gives no reply,

And its peaks and valleys remain dumb.

Turning back to the white lake for help,

And the magic tree in the center as well,

But Lord Dong still fails to find an answer,

From either the lake or the mighty tree.

Unable to hold back a flood of tears,

Dong shouts out his doubt against the sky:

"Could it be possible that my dear son

Has already been killed by the enemy?"

The shout meets waves rushing over the lake,

And clouds that roll and glide across the sky.

The shout spreads far to Luochi and Luosha,

Lord Dong's grandsons living on the enemy's land.

Trying to avoid seizure by the black clouds,

And avoid being seen by the black winds,

The two brothers succeed in fleeing away,

And meet their grandfather on the white land.

黑白之战 // The War Between the Black and the White Tribes

孙子见祖父,
呜呜哭不休。
孤儿好伤心,
草木也悲愁:

"父亲阿璐呵,
被术杀死了;
母亲茨嫫呵,
跟着爹去了。"

东主哭起来,
金嫫哭起来,
龙王哭起来,
鱼虾哭起来。

东主气难忍,
眼里迸火花,
好像雷击顶,
痛得虎样跳:

"我养九个男,
没有阿璐能;

祖孙相逢
The Reunion of Lord Dong's Family

When meeting their paternal grandpa,

The two children burst into bitter weeping;

As orphans without love from their parents,

They look woeful even to the lifeless trees:

"Ahlu, our beloved kindhearted dad

Was killed because of Shu's order;

And Cimo, our courageous mother,

Killed herself to keep him company."

Lord Dong fails to hold back his streaming tears,

His wife Jinmo bursts into bitter sobbing,

His dragon takes to sympathetic weeping,

And his fish and prawns also shed tears.

Finding it hard to control his rage,

Lord Dong beams out sparks from his red eyes;

As if stricken by a lightning flash,

He jumps high up like a burnt tiger:

"I have brought up nine sons altogether,

But none is as competent as Ahlu;

黑白之战 // The War Between the Black and the White Tribes

我育九个女,
没有阿璐美。

"不吃甜麦子,
吃着毒草了;
不进亲戚家,
进到仇家了。

"可悲歪天下,
躺着东族人;
可恨斜地下,
埋着能干人。

"日月般的脸,
怎能再看见?
宝石般的手,
怎能再摇晃?

"白玉般的心,
怎能再跳动?
星辰般的眼,
怎能再闪烁?"

祖孙相逢
The Reunion of Lord Dong's Family

I have raised nine daughters altogether,

Yet none is as handsome as Ahlu.

"Like a grazing ox on the pasture,

Ahlu ate noxious weeds by mistake;

Like a missionary on a long journey,

He stayed for a night at the wrong inn.

"Behold the dreadful scene under Shu's sky,

Where fighters from Dong's tribe lie in death;

Behold the bitter view on Shu's land,

Where warriors from Dong's tribe are buried.

"Those faces as fair as the sun and the moon.

Can they be seen again in this world?

Those hands as smooth as gem and jade.

Can they beckon again to their friends?

"Those hearts of our slaughtered neighbors,

Can they throb as they did when alive?

Those shining eyes of our dead kinsmen,

Can they blink like the stars in the sky?"

黑白之战 // The War Between the Black and the White Tribes

白的天哭了，

白的地哭了，

白的风哭了，

白的云哭了。

祖孙相逢
The Reunion of Lord Dong's Family

The sky of the White Tribe is shedding tears,

The land of the White Tribe is snivelling,

The wind of the White Tribe is whimpering,

And even its clouds are blubbering.

东术决战

The Decisive Battle

黑白之战 // The War Between the Black and the White Tribes

东将来请战,
东兵来请战:
像蝶围老树,
要去围术主。

有血流快了,
有心变热了。
东主召兵将,
商量大决战。

萨利委登呵,
来当东军师;
叶世恒丁呵,
派去搬天兵。

委登变三变,
铁块落下天。
请来好铁匠,
赶做刀和剑。

打铁像雷震,

东术决战
The Decisive Battle

Wishing to take a revenge on the enemy,

Dong's warriors come to him for orders;

Like butterflies flying around an aged tree,

They vow to surround Shu in a tight circle.

Their blood flows in a quicker manner,

And their hearts throb faster when soothed;

Coming together at Lord Dong's summons,

They make a sound plan for the fight.

Sali Weideng, at Lord Dong's appointment,

Serves as a consultant to his army;

Yeshi Hengding, at Dong's arrangement,

Goes as a courier to heaven for help.

Doing three times of witchcraft to the sky,

Weideng obtains iron bars from heaven;

Collecting good smiths across the land,

He urges them to make knives and swords.

Striking the bars in thundering clangs,

黑白之战 // The War Between the Black and the White Tribes

手杆像麻林，
风箱像虎吼，
火花像飞鹰。

砍下杜鹃树，
树枝削尖矛，
树皮做头盔，
树尖做刀把。

砍下铁杉树，
剖开做箭杆；
捉来白雪鸡，
做成羽翎箭。

犏牛和牦牛，
宰了千万双。
牛角做长弓，
牛皮做弓弦。

砍下岩竹来，
割下岩藤来，
剖竹做篾甲，
编藤做盾牌。

东术决战
The Decisive Battle

The smiths raise their arms like hemp stalks.

Their bellows roar like angry tigers,

And their sparks fly about like eagles.

Making use of azaleas from the hills,

They cut the branches into sharp spears:

The bark is made into strong helmets,

And the tree tops into knife handles.

Making use of hemlocks from the hills,

They split their trunks into arrow shafts;

Capturing pheasants from the bushes,

They use their feathers as fletchery.

Countless oxen and yaks are killed,

For the dried beef needed in the war;

The yak horns are made into fine bows,

And the ox hide into rawhide strings.

Bamboo is cut down from the hillsides,

And rattan is cut down from the cliffs;

The former is woven into armor,

While the latter is formed into shield.

黑白之战 // The War Between the Black and the White Tribes

恒丁变三变，
上天请兵将。
天将似雄狮，
天马似大象。

优麻①爱光明，
优麻请来了；
电神恨黑暗，
电神请来了。

白风去侦探，
术地杀气荡：
八十一个寨，
屯满黑鬼怪。

白云去巡察，
术地兵如麻。
黑石砌城堡，
砌了九个堡。

金蜂去查天，

---

① 优麻：护法神。

东术决战
The Decisive Battle

Doing three times of witchcraft to the sky,

Hengding sends for troops from heaven;

Their commanders are as brave as lions,

And their horses as strong as elephants.

Renowned for his love of brightness,

Youma① gets an honorary invitation;

Renowned for his hatred of darkness,

The God of Lightning also gets invited.

When the Wind goes for intelligence,

He sees a wave of wrath on Shu's land:

Garrisoned in the eighty-one camps

Are crowds of bellicose war mongers.

When the Cloud glides by on patrol,

He sees countless fighters on Shu's land;

Rocks are used to build defensive fortresses,

And nine fortresses are constructed in all.

When the Bee goes out to survey Shu's sky,

---

① Youma is the Protector of Justice in heaven.

黑白之战 // The War Between the Black and the White Tribes

术天黑云翻。
兽怪千百个，
死守大寨前。

蝙蝠去探路，
术路脚难踩。
铜棘像竹笋，
铁铡像石滩。

优麻磕牙齿，
天空巨雷轰；
优麻伸舌头，
天空现彩虹。

优麻竖竖尾，
高峰刮大风；
优麻翘翘胡，
魔鬼被吓懵。

优麻一怒吼，
术天发了抖。
好像面筛子，
上下抖不休。

东术决战
The Decisive Battle

He finds it full of dark rolling clouds;

Standing on guard in front of the camps,

The Griffins vow to fight to their last breath.

Going out to check Shu's road transportation,

The Bat finds it hard to walk on the roads;

For they are planted with copper thorns,

Or with pebble-like iron choppers.

When Youma grits and grinds his teeth,

The sound he makes cracks like thunder;

When Youma puts out his red tongue,

The sight he creates looks like a rainbow.

When Youma shows and curls up his tail,

The wind he makes whirls across the peaks;

When Youma raises his bushy whiskers,

Shu's monsters are frightened nearly to death.

When Youma gives out a fierce yell,

He puts Shu's sky to a continual shake,

Like a shifter

Used for flour grinding.

黑白之战 // The War Between the Black and the White Tribes

优麻一眨眼,
术地打寒战。
好像打摆子,
摇摆又晃荡。

天上隆隆响,
地上尘土扬。
东兵追术兵,
好像赶山羊。

金头白肚狮,
咬断黑龙腰,
术主九个堡,
破了第一堡;

绿壳穿山甲,
穿透黑虎腰,
术主九个堡,
破了第二堡;

孔雀张翅膀,
叼起黑蛇甩,

东术决战
The Decisive Battle

When Youma blinks and flashes his eyes,

He sends Shu's land to a terrible shiver,

Like a man who catches malaria,

Swinging and shaking.

Rumbling thunder is heard in the sky,

And whirling dust is seen on the land;

When Dong's soldiers chase after Shu's men,

It seems as if they were herding their goats.

A lion with a golden head and a white belly,

Breaks the middle part of the black dragon.

Of the nine fortresses built by Shu's men,

The first one is thus overtaken.

A pangolin with green and sharp shells,

Cuts through the waist of the black tiger.

Of the nine fortresses built by Shu's men,

The second one is thus occupied.

A peacock spreading his powerful wings,

Grabs and flings about the black viper.

术主第三堡,
转眼化黑烟;

金虎大爪子,
压扁赤眼鬼,
术主第四堡,
转眼化土堆;

银头白云豹,
咬死铁头狗,
术主第五堡,
塌成一条沟;

白铁神錾子,
錾倒石头门,
术主第六堡,
塌成一摊灰;

白螺雕宝弓,
射死黑甲魔,
术主第七堡,
像灶砸了锅;

东术决战
The Decisive Battle

Of the nine fortresses built by Shu's men,

The third one is turned into soot.

A golden tiger with giant and rough paws,

Crushes and squashes the red-eyed ghost.

Of the nine fortresses built by Shu's men,

The fourth one is turned into a mound.

A clouded leopard with a silver head,

Bites and puts the steel-headed dog to death.

Of the nine fortresses built by Shu's men,

The fifth one tumbles into a ditch.

A magic chisel made of white iron

Is employed to demolish the stone gate.

Of the nine fortresses built by Shu's men,

The sixth one is dissolved to ash.

A bow embedded with white conch shells

Is used to shoot Shu's monsters to death.

Of the nine fortresses built by Shu's men,

The seventh becomes a hearth without a pot.

黑白之战 // The War Between the Black and the White Tribes

白铁砍天刀,
斩断黑旋风,
术主第八堡,
好像雪山崩;

锋利神铁锯,
锯死黑角牛,
术主第九堡,
像灯尽了油。

刀剑像星星,
长矛像浪潮,
箭镞像下雨,
杀鬼像切瓜。

东兵和东将,
源源不断来,
狂风扫落叶,
术寨一扫光。

一将骑白虎,
斩了鹿头怪。
东兵涌上前,

东术决战
The Decisive Battle

A sky cutter made of white iron

Is used to cut off the black cyclone.

Of the nine fortresses built by Shu's men,

The eighth one crashes like avalanche.

A sharp saw made of quality iron

Is used to mow down the black-horned ox.

Of the nine fortresses built by Shu's men,

The last runs out of fuel like an oil lamp.

With their swords as glittering as stars,

Their spears as powerful as torrents,

And their arrows as dense as showers,

Dong's men cut their enemies like melons.

Generals and soldiers from the White Tribe,

Keep rushing to the battle in a stream.

Like leaves swept away by a strong wind,

Shu's fortresses are pulled down in a wink.

A general riding a white tiger,

Beheads the deer-headed monster;

Attacking the enemy in a large number,

黑白之战 // The War Between the Black and the White Tribes

破了鹿骨寨。

一将骑金象，
斩了牛头怪。
东兵涌上前，
破了牛骨寨。

一将骑白狮，
斩了马头怪。
东兵涌上前，
破了马骨寨。

一将骑白狼，
斩了羊头怪。
东兵涌上前，
破了羊骨寨。

一将骑豹子，
斩了狗头怪。
东兵涌上前，
破了狗骨寨。

一将骑神鹏，

东术决战
The Decisive Battle

His men seize the deer-boned fort.

A general riding an elephant,

Beheads the ox-headed monster;

Attacking the enemy in a large number,

His men seize the ox-boned fort.

A general riding a white lion,

Beheads the horse-headed monster;

Attacking the enemy in a large number,

His men seize the horse-boned fort.

A general riding a white wolf,

Beheads the goat-headed monster;

Attacking the enemy in a large number,

His men seize the goat-boned fort.

The general riding a leopard,

Beheads the dog-headed monster;

Attacking the enemy in a large number,

His men seize the dog-boned fort.

The general riding a magic hawk,

斩了鸡头怪。

东兵涌上前，

破了鸡骨寨。

一将骑水獭，

斩了蛙头怪。

东兵涌上前，

破了蛙骨寨。

一将骑金獐，

斩了蛇头怪。

东兵涌上前，

破了蛇骨寨。

一将骑大鳖，

斩了鱼头怪。

东兵涌上前，

破了鱼骨寨。

放出白风云，

压住黑风云；

放出金翅鸟，

吞了黑鹊鸟。

东术决战
The Decisive Battle

Beheads the rooster-headed monster;

Attacking the enemy in a great number,

His men seize the rooster-boned fort.

The general riding a giant otter,

Beheads the frog-headed monster;

Attacking the enemy in a great number,

His men seize the frog-boned fort.

The general riding a roebuck,

Beheads the snake-headed monster;

Attacking the enemy in a great number,

His men seize the snake-boned fort.

The general riding a huge turtle,

Beheads the fish-headed monster;

Attacking the enemy in a great number,

His men seize the fish-boned fort.

Sending out his mystic winds and clouds,

Dong takes control of Shu's winds and clouds;

Releasing his flock of gold-winged hawks,

He urges them to gobble up Shu's magpies.

黑白之战 // The War Between the Black and the White Tribes

放出白铁斧,

砍尽黑铁桩;

放出白梭镖,

凿穿术水塘。

东兵到东方,

杀九个木鬼,

斩当饶吉补①,

破了木堡垒;

东兵到南方,

杀九个火鬼,

斩时知吉补,

破了火堡垒;

东兵到西方,

杀九个铁鬼,

斩勒钦斯普,

破了铁堡垒;

---

① 当饶吉补及后面所列的时知吉补、勒钦斯普、奴朱吉补、米麻生登,分别为东南西北中五方鬼王。

东术决战
The Decisive Battle

Sending out his gigantic iron axes,

Dong hacks away at Shu's iron stakes;

Casting his dart in a horizontal way,

He pokes it through Shu's water pond.

Driving some enemies to the east,

Dong's fighters kill nine wooden monsters;

Killing the chieftain Dangrao Jibu[①],

They take over the wooden blockhouse.

Driving some enemies to the south,

Dong's fighters kill nine fire monsters;

Killing the chieftain Shizhi Jibu,

They take over the fire blockhouse.

Driving some enemies to the west,

Dong's fighters kill nine iron monsters;

Killing the chieftain Leqin Sipu,

They take over the iron blockhouse.

---

① Dangrao Jibu, Shizhi Jibu, Leqin Sipu, Nuzhu Jibu and Mima Shengdeng are kings of monsters in the east, the south, the west, the north and the center of the world.

黑白之战 // The War Between the Black and the White Tribes

东兵到北方,
杀九个水鬼,
斩奴朱吉补,
破了水堡垒;

东兵到中央,
杀九个土鬼,
斩米麻生登,
破了土堡垒。

金头白猿猴,
挥斧捉凶首。
术主拿住了,
纳嫫拿住了。

砍了术的兵,
宰了术的马;
丹由逃不了,
左普逃不了!

烧毁术的城,
冲毁术的地,
灭掉术的火,

东术决战
The Decisive Battle

Driving some enemies to the north,
Dong's fighters kill nine water monsters;
Killing the chieftain Nuzhu Jibu,
They take over the water blockhouse.

Driving some enemies to the middle,
Dong's fighters kill nine earthen monsters;
Killing the chieftain Mima Shengdeng,
They take over the earthen blockhouse.

General Monkey with a golden head,
Captures the culprits with his huge axe:
Shu is taken as a prisoner of war,
And Namo as a prisoner too.

Shu's soldiers are punished to death,
And his horses are butchered for meat;
His generals have nowhere to flee,
Including of Danyou and Zuopu!

The towns on Shu's land are burnt down,
The farmlands on Shu's land are flooded,
The fires in Shu's households are wiped out,

黑白之战 // The War Between the Black and the White Tribes

截断术的水。

敏锐黑眼睛,
挖掉不留它;
能飞黑翅膀,
削掉不留它。

会射黑手腕,
割掉不留下;
善跑黑脚杆,
砍掉不留下。

割下术主头,
雕成纪功碑;
取下术主骨,
镂成号角吹。

术地翻做天,
术天割做地。
术狗不吠了,
术鸡不啼了。

宰牲祭先烈,

东术决战
The Decisive Battle

And even the water supply is cut off.

The sharp eyes of Shu's defeated soldiers
Are dug out to get rid of their fighting force;
The black flying wings of Shu's monsters
Are cut off to get rid of their fighting force.

The deft wrists of Shu's defeated soldiers
Are cut off to get rid of their fighting force;
The black running legs of the prisoners
Are cut off to get rid of their fighting force.

Part of the skull taken from Shu's head,
Is used to record Dong's victory;
Part of the shank taken from Shu's leg,
Is carved into a bugle as a proud trophy.

Shu's land is turned up to be the sky,
And his sky is chopped into the land;
His dogs are no longer heard to bark,
And his roosters no longer heard to crow.

Shu's animals are killed as sacrifices

黑白之战 // The War Between the Black and the White Tribes

超荐阿璐灵；
燃柏做祈祷，
超荐茨嫫魂。

圣香驱秽气，
圣水洗妖腥。
符咒压魔鬼，
永世难翻身。

东术决战
The Decisive Battle

To save Ahlu's soul from purgatory;

The cypress trunks are burnt for prayers

To save Cimo's soul from purgatory.

The noxious gas is smoked with incense,

And the ghost scent is washed with water;

Shu's monsters are buried with amulets

To prevent their rebirth in the future.

光明永存
The Eternity of Light

黑白之战 // The War Between the Black and the White Tribes

黑道无人助，
白道众心归。
黑道地底沉，
光明天上升。

用升量珠宝，
用柜装金银。
厚礼献优麻，
犒劳天神兵。

天兵回天宫，
百姓庆凯旋。
大碗喝热奶，
大盅饮酒浆。

篝火烧起来，
鼓乐奏起来，
千人舞起来，
万众唱起来：

"豺狼闯羊圈，

光明永存
The Eternity of Light

Lord Shu loses supports due to his bad behavior,
While Lord Dong gains favors with his lofty deeds;
Shu's land sinks to the bottom of the earth,
While bright light arises over Dong's land.

Lord Dong measures his jewelry with liters,
And stores his treasures in large boxes;
He awards Youma with lavish gifts,
And treats his heavenly troops to grand feasts.

The heavenly troops return with great honors,
While Dong's men celebrate their triumphs;
They gulp down warm milk from large bowls,
And booze up good liquor from huge pots.

Campfires are burnt for the party,
And drums are beat for the party;
They do group dancing to the rhythm,
And chorus singing around the campfires:

"When the jackals enter the sheepfold,

黑白之战 // The War Between the Black and the White Tribes

自我坟墓埋;
术魔逞凶狂,
自投黑罗网。

"白鹿脱虎爪,
白羊脱狼爪,
白雀脱鹰爪,
白鱼脱獭爪。

"东族得胜利,
焦山又绿遍;
光明得胜利,
千河又淌满。

"太阳更温暖,
月亮更清朗,
松柏千年翠,
泉水万年甜!"

白的天笑了,
白的地笑了,
白的风笑了,
白的云笑了。

光明永存
The Eternity of Light

They are to incur peril to themselves;

When the monsters perform ruthless acts,

They are to put themselves in a danger.

"Dong's deer bump away from the tigers,

His sheep run away from the fierce wolves,

His sparrows fly away from the eagles,

And his fish swim away from otters.

"Ever since his victory over h..

Lord Dong sees green trees covering

While bright sunshine lights up the land,

Fresh water keeps running in the streams.

"The sun has becomes warmer than before,

And the moon much clearer and more serene;

Cypress trees remain lush and green year round,

And sweet water keeps running from the fountains!"

The sky seems to be laughing in the light,

The land seems to be merry with the crops,

The winds seem to giggle through the trees,

And the clouds seem to grin over the sky.

黑白之战 // The War Between the Black and the White Tribes

天空平展展，
天空亮堂堂；
大鹏翩翩飞，
白鹤自在鸣。

大地像金毯，
六畜像金丸，
五谷像珍珠，
遍地滚起来。

高山高岩间，
百鸟唱得欢，
百兽跳得欢，
百花开得欢。

大海深湖里，
银龙戏碧水；
水下结珠贝，
水上鱼成队。

黑风不敢犯，
魔气不敢缠。

光明永存
The Eternity of Light

The white sky extends far into the distance,

And the sky becomes shiny in bright hues;

The hawks soar high in a graceful way,

And the cranes scream in a gleeful way.

The autumn fields look like golden blankets,

The livestock on the pasture moves like golden balls,

And the grains of the crops look like pearls,

All sweeping across the land in the winds.

On the mountain slopes and steep cliffs,

Birds are heard to sing songs in chorus,

Wild beasts are seen to put on a dance,

And flowers are blooming in their prime.

In the deep bottom of the white lake,

A silvery dragon plays with the water;

Pearls grow in bunches at the bottom,

And schools of fish swim near the surface.

The black wind blows not across the border,

And the noxious air brings people no disease.

黑白之战 // The War Between the Black and the White Tribes

高碑刻平安,

大路皆康庄。

干戈化锦绣,

剑火化香甜。

吃的堆成山,

穿的铺成海。

少男和少女,

有了好婚姻;

老翁和老妇,

得了好寿岁。

雪山年年白,

东族代代传;

鲜花开不败,

东族永不衰。

金线绣太阳,

银线绣月亮,

玉线绣星星,

七星①闪异彩。

---

① 七星:指绣饰在纳西妇女披肩上的七个彩色圆盘。

光明永存
The Eternity of Light

The peaceful events are inscribed on the high stele,

And the roads are now safe for travel.

Tribal hatred is replaced by friendship,

And fighting arms are replaced with handshakes.

Stacks of grain are put up in towering piles,

And heaps of clothing are wider than the lake.

Having the freedom to date their lovers,

The young enjoy well-matched marriages;

Living happier and healthier lives,

The elderly people grow to advanced ages.

Like the hills blessed with snow year after year,

The White Tribe keeps thriving for generations;

Like the red plum that blooms the year round,

The White Tribe remains prosperous forever.

Golden threads are used to adorn the sun,

Silver threads are used to adorn the moon,

Jade threads are used to adorn the stars,

黑白之战 // The War Between the Black and the White Tribes

太阳千秋照,

月亮千秋亮,

星星千秋明,

光明千秋在。

光明永存
The Eternity of Light

So the Seven-Star① glitters in the light.

The sun gives off its eternal radiance,
The moon gives off its eternal radiance,
The stars give off its eternal radiance,
And they all help to light up Dong's land.

---

① The Seven-Star refers to the seven colored plates that are embroidered on the shawls of the Naxi women.

译后记

《黑白之战》是我国纳西族神话史诗。这部长篇英雄史诗与《创世纪》和《鲁般鲁饶》并称纳西东巴文学的"三颗明珠"。该诗被完整地记载于纳西族东巴经籍中,东巴文称"东埃术埃",直译是"东术仇斗",即东部落与术部落的战争。该诗不仅是纳西文学的巅峰之作,同时也被公认为我国南方少数民族英雄史诗的典范之作。

该诗产生的历史背景是纳西族先民社会从父权制向奴隶制转化的过渡阶段。该诗通过描写"黑""白"两个部落之间为争夺代表光明的"日、月"而进行的部族战争,深刻揭示"白界战胜黑界、光明战胜黑暗"的主题,彰显人类社会"邪不压正"的伦理道义。

《黑白之战》汉语版本较多,此次英译采用的源文本是由著名的纳西族学者杨世光汉译、云南人民出版社2009年出版的版本。该版本结构紧凑严谨,层次分明,矛盾集中;情节引人入胜,依次展开,渐至高潮；主要包括"争战起源、米委丧生、术兵犯境、东术决战"等内容，其环环相扣，跌宕起伏，一气呵成。该版本充分展示了原作者匠心独运的情节构思、大胆稔熟的艺术手法以及引人入胜的叙事能力。

全诗共有20章487节，形式每节为近体五言四行，语言简明，韵律灵活。为顺应当今社会主流诗学"理念颤变"和目标语读者"兴趣转向"，我们翻译时采用"非韵体翻译"，以追求原诗意境再现为旨要，确保译文"轻重交迭、长短整齐"。

本译著由3位译者合作完成。主译孙兴文教授负责"天地初始"到"术主寻衅"共8章初译；第二译者贾丽丽负责"术兵犯境"至"光明永存"共7章初译；第三译者罗慧凡负责"遣兵侦察"至"身陷魔窟"共5章初译。全书统稿、校改由主译完成。

孙兴文

Translators' Afterword

The War Between the Black and the White Tribes is a heroic epic created in the age of mythology by the Naxi ethnic group in China. It is viewed as one of "The Three Pearls" in Naxi literature, with the other two being *Genesis* and *Luban Lurao*. It is recorded in the Dongba sutras of the Naxi people, with the phonetic name of *Dong'ai Shu'ai* in their old hieroglyphic language which means in Chinese *Dong-Shu Freud* or in English "The War Between the Black and the White Tribes". It is acknowledged not only as a literary masterpiece in Naxi literature but also a representative of its genre for all the ethnic groups living in south China.

This epic was created by Naxi ancestors in the transition stage when their society was undergoing changes from patriarchy to slavery. Through a vivid description of the war between the Black and the White tribes over the sun and the moon that stand for brightness, it provides an exposition of the universal theme that "white wins over black and bright over dark". It also demonstrates the moral principle that "evil can never prevail over good".

From multiple versions in Chinese that are currently

available, the most authentic was singled out as the source for our translation project. The text was collated and translated from Naxi into Chinese by Mr. Yang Shiguang, a renowned scholar of Naxi culture and published in April, 2009 by Yunnan People's Publishing House. Several distinctive features are identified in Yang's version, such as a rigorous design of structure, a plausible knit of layers, a focused grid of conflicts, an appealing array of plots, an orderly unveiling of scenes, and an ascending approach to climaxes. The major stories in the book, such as "The Brewing of the War", "The Theft by Lord Shu", "The Death of Miwei", "The Invasion of Shu's Soldiers" and "The Decisive Battle", are told in a consecutive, winding yet interlocking manner. It obviously reflects the author's outstanding talent in plot conception, use of rhetoric devices, not to mention the appealing way for story telling.

We find altogether 20 cantos or 487 stanzas in Yang's Chinese version of *The War Between the Black and the White Tribes*. They are exclusively composed in a modern style using plain words and flexible rhythm, with five characters in each of the four lines in a stanza. They are translated into English in the form of unrhymed verse to cope with the "conceptual change" in the dominant practice of composing modern poems, and the "interest shift" of our prospective readership in English-speaking countries. The manifold purpose of such an approach is to transplant the original imagery on the one hand, and to achieve the function of "rhythmic intervals of stressed and unstressed syllables and equivalent lengths of poetic lines".

This is a work jointly accomplished by three translators. Professor Sun Xingwen, the chief translator, translated the first eight cantos from "The Beginning of the World" to "The Provoking of Lord Shu". Ms. Jia Lili, the second translator, translated the last seven cantos from "The Invasion of Shu's Soldiers" to "The Eternity of Light". Ms. Luo Huifan, the third translator, translated five cantos in the middle part from "The Spying of the Situation" to "The Trapping of Ahlu". The whole draft was revised and polished by the chief translator.

Sun Xingwen

译者简介

孙兴文，云南师范大学外国语学院英语教授。迄今已在各类刊物发表学术论文28篇，主持科研项目5项。近年出版物主要有4部著作：《中国竹类》（国际竹藤组织，2010年）、《从管约理论到最简方案：句法理论与句子分析》（科学出版社，2010年）、《撒都语研究》（美国学术出版社，2015年）、《搓梭语研究》（美国学术出版社，2018年）。主要研究兴趣：英语语言学及英汉互译研究。

贾丽丽，四川外国语大学成都学院讲师，曾是云南师范大学外国语学院2011级翻译硕士研究生。已在《牡丹江教育学院学报》《湖北教育学院学报》《齐齐哈尔师范专科学校学报》等刊物发表学术论文7篇，参与过《撒都语研究》（美国学术出版社，2015年）一书翻译。主要研究兴趣：英汉互译理论与实践研究。

罗慧凡，丽江师范高等专科学校讲师，曾是云南师范大学外国语学院2015级翻译硕士研究生。曾获得2016年昆明"南亚博览会翻译大赛"二等奖，主持2014年云南省哲社青年项目"纳西族叙事长诗《玉龙第三国》英译及研究"，已在各类刊物发表学术论文10篇。主要研究兴趣：云南少数民族典籍英译研究。

About the Translators

Sun Xingwen is a professor of English in the School of Foreign Languages and Literature at Yunnan Normal University. Up to now he has published 28 academic papers published in various journals and hosted 5 research programs. His recent major publications include 4 books: *Bamboos in China* (International Network for Bamboo and Rattan, 2010), *From GB to MP: Syntax Theories and Sentence Analyses* (Science Press, 2010), *A Study of the Sadu Language* (American Academic Press, 2015), and *A Study of the Cuosuo Language* (American Academic Press, 2018). His research interests focus on English linguistics and research in mutual translation between English and Chinese.

Jia Lili is a lecturer of English at Chengdu Institute of Sichuan International Studies University. In 2011 she was enrolled for a 3-year study in the program of Master of Translation and Interpreting (MTI) by the School of Foreign Languages and Literature at Yunnan Normal University. Up to now she has published 7 academic papers in various journals such as The Journal of Mudanjiang College of Education, The Journal of Hubei University of Education, and The Journal of

Qiqihar Teachers College. She also took part in the translation of *A Study of the Sadu Language* (American Academic Press, 2015). Her research interests focus on theories and practices in mutual translation between Chinese and English.

Luo Huifan is a lecturer of English at Lijiang Teachers College. She was also an MTI student who began her 3-year study starting from 2015 in the School of Foreign Languages and Literature at Yunnan Normal University. She won a 2nd prize in the China-South Asia Expo Translation Contest held in Kunming in 2016. She hosted The English Translation and Study of the Naxi Epic "The Wonderland of Yulong Snow Mountain", a research project approved by Yunnan Provincial Planning Office of Philosophy and Social Sciences in 2014. Up to now she has published 10 academic papers in various journals. Her research interests focus on the English translation of ethnic classics in Yunnan Province.